Sir Norman the Cat

GW00541499

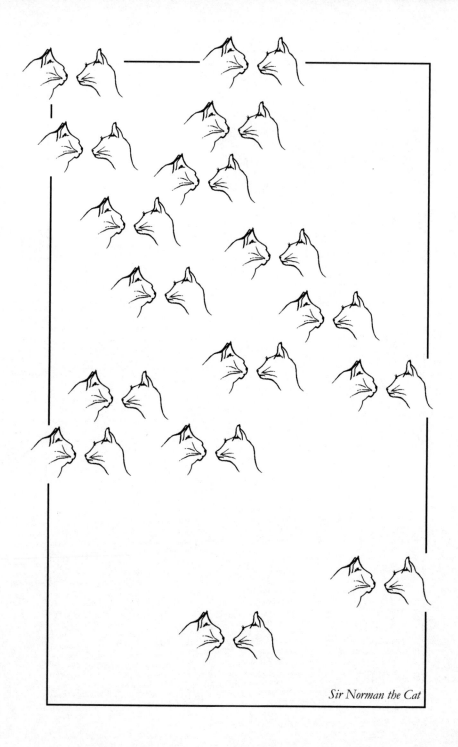

Sir Norman the Cat

Sir Norman the Cat

Letters from a once-traumatised cat

by Antonella Cane

*Sir Norman the Cat's story is about one small animal's
will to survive and demonstrates how courage
and determination can surmount daunting obstacles*

www.SirNorman.com

Wild Berry & Friends

Editions Wild Berry & Friends
Edenbridge, Kent, UK and Robilante-Farm, Italy

I dedicate this book to my dearest and beloved sister Christiane. And to Burela.

My warmest and deepest thanks to Nico and Roy, Val and Melissa, without whom Norman would not be Sir Norman the Cat. And a very special thank you to Sally Adams, Judith Bayley, Judy Hartley, Gillian Morrison-Baxter and Barbara Williams.

My highest recognition to Alan F. Sundberg for his art direction and design, and the book project management by his Ringfort Studios, Berlin and Venice.

A. C., August 2005

Impressum

Editions Wild Berry & Friends
(Antonella Cane)
P.O. Box 134, Edenbridge,
Kent TN8 9AF UK

...and Robilante-Farm, Italy. Visit us online at: www.SirNorman.com

Art direction and design by Alan F. Sundberg/Ringfort Studio,
www.RingfortStudio.com

Manufactured in the United Kingdom by Antony Rowe Ltd., East Sussex

10 9 8 7 6 5 4 3 2 1

British Library - Cataloguing in Publication CIP Data: a catalogue
record for this book is available from the British Library:

Cane, Antonella.
   'Sir Norman the Cat: letters from a
   once-traumatised cat'/ Antonella Cane   p. cm.
   'Editions Wild Berry & Friends (Antonella Cane)'
   1. Norman, Sir – Parodies, imitations, etc. 2. Animals,
   pets, cats and children stories, Italian/British.
   I. Title: 'Sir Norman the Cat: letters from a
   once-traumatised cat'. II. Cane, Antonella, date. III. Title.

ISBN 0-9550803-1-2

Foreword

The story of Sir Norman chronicles one small cat's triumph over enormous adversity. It is a story about the will to survive and demonstrates how courage and determination can surmount daunting obstacles. Sir Norman suffered devastating injuries when he was hit by a car and initially it appeared that he would never recover from the trauma. He was found by a Good Samaritan who brought him to us to try to repair his broken body. The initial assessment revealed he had a badly broken pelvis and both back legs were paralysed. The damage to the bones of his pelvis could be repaired with steel pins and wires but damaged nerves cannot be repaired. Only time would tell if the nerve damage would recover sufficiently for him to ever be able to walk again. He was a stray cat and no one came forward to claim him as their pet. He was lost and alone and it was unlikely that he would ever walk again – we all feared the worst.

The dilemma was whether it was morally right to subject him to major surgery because he had only a very slim chance of ever regaining the ability to walk. Despite tremendous pain, Sir Norman's character and resilience won the hearts of the staff at the veterinary clinic who agreed to do everything in their power to give him the best possible chance of recovery. Despite both back legs being paralysed, his personality sparkled and his appetite for food was enormous. He seemed unconcerned that he couldn't walk and seemed interested only in food and the fuss and attention lavished on him. We performed the surgery at the clinic and repaired the damage to the pelvic bones. He recovered very well from the operation and from the moment he opened his eyes it was clear to us that his appetite was certainly unaffected by the surgery. He lived with us at the clinic for several weeks while we watched and waited to see if his back legs would ever work again. He seemed quite content to drag himself around with his front legs and as a result he developed very large and powerful shoulders. He greeted everyone with a good spirited chirrup every time we walked by and begged unashamedly for as much food as he could get.

After a few weeks we noticed very small movements in the back legs and as the weeks passed the movements became stronger and more controlled. One day he used the power in his shoulders to hoist his lower back off the ground, but he was still unable to use his back legs. This was a turning point and every day he kept improving until he started to bear some weight on his back legs. The back end was still very wobbly but it seemed he would gain enough function to be able to get around and live a contented and comfort

5

able life. It was at this stage that we wondered where he was going to live. All of us at the clinic already had many pets and we didn't think he could fit in with our pets. One day, Antonella Cane, an Italian lady, came to visit us at the clinic and we discussed Sir Norman's miraculous recovery with her. Antonella already had two adult female cats at home called Pirate and Black Gold and the question was whether they would accept a newcomer to the Cane family. After extensive thought and deliberation, Antonella agreed to take Sir Norman home and see how he would be received. We gave her strict instructions that Sir Norman was to be confined at all times because he still had a long way to go to recover from his injuries and it was important that he didn't overexert himself.

One day a fax appeared on our fax machine from Sir Norman *himself*, giving us an update on his progress and describing life at his new home. He sounded very happy and his medical progress was remarkable. He started sending us regular faxes describing his adventures and his integration into his new kingdom. Each letter touched our hearts and etched smiles on our faces. His exploits and achievements were described with such zeal and enthusiasm that we decided we should share this story with the entire world. We asked Antonella to ensure that Sir Norman kept writing and suggested that his letters be published. Antonella, acting as Sir Norman's assistant, has collected his letters and they are presented to you as his memoirs in this book. Each letter is a delight to read on its own and collectively the letters chart his progress as he recovered from his mental and physical trauma, to develop into the enormous personality that is Sir Norman.

Today Sir Norman lives a full and active life and insists he is landed gentry. He has so much personal magnetism and his persona is so much larger than life that no one has disputed his claim to heraldry and title. His *knighthood* has been bestowed on him by all that is good in this world in recognition of his achievements. Long live Sir Norman the Cat.

Nico Maritz, Surrey, UK

A series of letters by a once-traumatised cat
to a place called 'Wild Berry'

This is your life. Once upon a time ... once-traumatised ... No, I'm no poet, I'm no writer – just a simple house cat. But I do write letters, simple, unpretentious letters. I write letters in which I would like to describe how I started in life, letters to keep all my friends informed about the many exciting things that are happening to me. I first started my life as if I was in a dream world, then I was rescued and the reality of life started ... after I was able to cope with my accident by writing funny things about it (doctors call this therapy: integration *vs* repression).

Life can be so exciting for a cat: you just need a little bit of imagination to start with, and then things start happening. I'm living proof of this, truly, you'll see by my letters.

Sir Norman the Cat

PS As my computer skills were not up to par, an Italian lady gave me a paw to help me type in English and send my messages to 'Wild Berry'.

Contents

1. Sekhmet, me, and Sekhmet's gifts

Good day,

I was given the name of Norman. Later on I'll tell you how I became *knighted* as Sir Norman. I have a great passion in life. Well, if I'm honest I'd say that really I have several. Guess what one of my great passions is? It's talking! I talk to my friends, my mum, I talk to my dad. I'd talk to my sisters too if only they'd listen, but they're just not interested so I end up talking to myself.

I just love chatting, I can't help it. I chat all the time. As talking is one of my passions and I have plenty of things to say, I'm going to talk to you now. I'm going to tell you a secret so please promise you won't give it away. I'm going to tell you what happened to me and how I was given the name of Norman! Seriously, honestly, I've got to tell someone.

I made everyone around me believe that only the elves and the fairies knew where I came from. But that's just because this is part of my secret – it's part of the magic!

Listen to this, I'll tell you too. One day I was found in a garden by the fairy Sekhmet, as she was passing by with a small army of elves. She stopped and took a look at me and shook her head. She stood there for a while and all she could do was shake her head – that's a lot of wasted time when one could say so much! Then all of a sudden she flew away. Needless to say she left me very disappointed as I had so many things to talk about, so many things to say to her. After a while I could hear something that sounded like the wings of a butterfly, but then I could hear harmonious tunes brought in by the wind so I knew it was no butterfly. It was Sekhmet and her elves. I got all agitated because I didn't want them to come Sekhmet, take one look at me and fly away like they did earlier. Remember, I had so much to tell them, so I started talking to them and told them that no way would they leave me alone a second time, no way! "Will you be quiet?" Sekhmet said all of a sudden in a bossy way. I was taken aback by the tone of her voice. She was so beautiful, I never thought she could order me to be quiet. But I did keep quiet. It took some effort though; I just had so much to tell her!

Now that I had to keep quiet, I kept saying to myself, "She is so beautiful, I wonder where she comes from?" I couldn't stop looking at her; I was convinced her eyes were made of diamonds. I was lost in my thoughts ... bliss. Then she ordered me to be quiet again. I was dreaming. Well, that's what I thought anyway. As I said, I talk so much that I didn't realise that even when I think I'm thinking, I talk out loud. She told me she had to leave me alone earlier because she needed to talk to the elves, she needed to ask them what she should do with me. I didn't know that, she was just explaining to me. Her voice was as beautiful as she was herself, so I just stood there staring at her.

During the meeting with the elves, Sekhmet was told that, because she was the one who found me, she should give me three gifts before letting me out into the big world. She thought a little, the elves thought a little, and then they all knew what I should be given. I mean, I wasn't at that meeting, I couldn't walk, let alone fly with the elves – I'm just repeating to you what Sekhmet told me. The first gift that Sekhmet told me she wanted to give me was a black and white coat. She said it would protect me and bring me good luck. Mind you, I had no idea of fashion. Even now I have no idea what I should wear. So I was given my coat and to this day I'm wearing it! I like it very much, it fits very well.

As a second gift, Sekhmet told me she wanted to give my eyes the colour of precious stones. To be perfectly honest, I've never looked at myself in a mirror so I had no idea what she was talking about, but I was immensely intrigued by what she was saying.

She looked at me for what felt like hours. It was embarrassing really, she was so beautiful, I couldn't understand why she was spending so much time looking at me in such a manner! All of a sudden she said, "Aquamarine, I will give your eyes the colour of aquamarine." I thought, whatever that might be, as long as it keeps her happy, it's OK with me.

Sekhmet told me that the third gift would be the most important one. I was so anxious to know what it would be and I was gathering all my strength to catch everything she was saying. (Oh, by the way, I never said a word for quite a while for I was scared to be told off again.) But by that time I was also so very tired. You see, I wanted to maintain a decent posture in front of beautiful Sekhmet so I kept myself presentable lying there in the garden on my arms and that was very tiring. I told you I got mixed up with the elves; they know everything, honest, you can't hide anything from an elf, much less so from Sekhmet. She knew I was getting tired and told me she'd explain about the third gift later.

Ooooohhhhhhhhh no, I said, don't want to sleep, no. But despite my protests, Sekhmet wouldn't say what the third gift was. I tried to plead with her but she sat next to me and told me I needed a little sleep, she told me she'd talk about the third gift when I woke up.

Before I knew it I was asleep. But somehow I knew Sekhmet remained next to me for I could see her in my sleep.

I'll tell you more later, bye for now.

Norman

(Sekhmet = Egyptian Mythology, the Lionness Goddess)

2. The third gift

Hello again,

I must have slept for two hours, maybe three. Maybe I slept for three days as it felt like such a long time!

Waking up near Sekhmet was such an experience, I started talking to her and trying to explain what happened to me but she said she was the one who was there to do the talking, not me. Oops, I did it again! She told me there was no need to tell her about myself as she had the magic power of knowing but, even more so, of loving and protecting and so she knew who I was; such a mystery to my little person!

Sekhmet told me the third gift was a place.

A place ... "Yes," she said. "A place. A place called Wild Berry."

So I say, "A place called Wild Berry?"

"Yes," she said.

I was waiting for Sekhmet to explain but she kept the mystery going and I was getting so confused. A place called Wild Berry, what on earth would they do in a place called Wild Berry? Jams?

That's it. They make jams, jelly, marmalade. I don't like jam, I don't eat jelly and I don't want to know about marmalade; why should I go there? All these questions were going round and round in my head. Sekhmet knew what was going on in my mind, she told me to calm down and told me that, more importantly, what I would find at Wild Berry instead of jam, jelly, or marmalade, was friends.

Friends?

"Yes, friends that will look after you," she said.

I thought a little and then said, "Never mind about that, will they talk to me? Will I be able to talk to them?" I needed to know that for sure, otherwise there was no point in continuing the conversation.

"Will I have friends that I can talk to? Yes or no?" I wanted to know at once.

Sekhmet shook her head and smiled at me, she said these friends would talk to me.

"Never mind about that, will they let ME talk? Yes or no? I need to know now." Talking is a vital part of my life so it was important to know at once whether these friends would let *me* talk to *them*. I was getting all agitated at the thought of going somewhere I would be kept quiet. Sekhmet smiled and told me not to worry, she had known these friends she was talking about for a long time and she said they'd be perfect friends who would love and protect me.

Don't know why but I felt such comfort in my heart. Not only was Sekhmet beautiful but she also spoke so well ... bliss. I felt like I wanted to jump up and put my arms around her neck and give her a purrrrrfect hug but my legs wouldn't let me reach up to her. Then I thought, maybe a small boy is better off not hugging a lady, maybe she wouldn't like me to put my arms around her neck. Maybe I shouldn't do such things anyway. All these points were going round in my mind at once, my head was spinning with what Sekhmet had said and with what I wanted to do. My arms, helping me to maintain my dignified posture, were getting heavy. Oh, it was so tiring, so very tiring, I was blushing. Sekhmet bent over me and planted a kiss on my pink nose and she told me not to worry about anything. Ooooooohhh, dearie, dearie me, my nose has been pink ever since!

I fell asleep.

I'll tell you more when I wake up, speak later.

Much love,
Norman

3. First, the place

Hello, I'm awake again!

I slept again for what felt like months, I was so exhausted, so very tired. I woke up, and opened my eyes but my brain still felt asleep. I can't wake up properly, I said to myself.; I wanted to start talking about so many things, I'd been quiet for so long, too long. I tried to get up and speak. I was convinced there must be someone around who'd listen, maybe even answer me. I made an effort to get up again but no way could I make it, I had to use my arms again to move around.

This moving around woke me up!

Geeeeeeee, I thought, I don't know this place. Where am I? I'm warm, it's all clean around me. I think I'm still sleeping, I can't possibly be awake, right? I'm asleep, having a dream, right?

I moved around a bit more. No, I'm awake, I thought, this is real!

Just a little more effort, a little more toward there, what's this? Oooohhhhh, smells nice. Hmmmmmm, not sure about it. Go on, a little more effort to see what's in there, smells real good. Wonder if I can have some? I feel quite peckish really, my tummy is rumbling.

BISCUITS!

Do you think they're for me? What if? Smells good. What if?

What if I get in trouble if I touch them? Surely there must be someone I can ask? Can ask, can ask, can ask? I'm ready to talk, I need to talk, I want to speak to someone!

H-E-L-L-O-OOOOOOOOOOOOO, anybody there?

H-E-L-L-O-OOOO can anyone hear me?
Not a sound! Well, a lot of noise because my belly was now really rumbling very loud, very very loud, and those biscuits were smelling so nice. Ooooohhhhhhh, never mind, I'll have some, I thought, I can't wait any longer. I'll be able to explain myself, I'm just too hungry, got to stop my tummy making so much noise before I get into trouble for being a nuisance.

Scrunch, scrunch, scrunch! These are really tasty. I wonder who left them there. Surely they can't be for me, right?! Ohhhhh, maybe I'm eating somebody's dinner. Gee, that means trouble. Never mind, just a little more ... they taste soooooo good.

Oh, well, that was nice! My tummy is no longer noisy, I can think better now!

A little look here, a little look there. Where am I? Never seen here before, never been here before, I wonder where I am. I think and I think and I think again, but I can't recall ever being here. I'm not that old so for sure I'm not losing my marbles yet, but I just can't remember this place. I've never seen such a good place before; clean, warm, beautiful, calm, really a good place. However, my brain is rattling because I can't remember this place, I just can't remember it. Because of my wandering, I've been to plenty of different gardens, sheds, garages, etc. but never in this place, such a posh place.

A place, a place, a place. THE PLACE! Can this be the place? For sure it must be? This is so posh, so beautiful, it must be the place that Sekhmet was talking about, right? I'm sure it is. Ooohhhh, I'm so excited, this is it, this is it, this is the place! But what if it's not? I shivered to think that maybe this wasn't the place Sekhmet talked about. But then some more harmonious tunes were coming through the window and I knew immediately Sekhmet was around! I couldn't wait to see her again. Where was she?

And all of a sudden there she was! Beautiful as ever!

She took a look at me, she wanted to make sure, she said, that I was still wearing my black and white coat.

"Of course I'm wearing it, I never had a proper coat before." And the one she gave me as a gift was so warm and shiny that I didn't want to let it go, so of course I was wearing it. Sekhmet went around checking the place, making sure everything was in good order. She then asked me if I had had something to eat and I said I found those biscuits, that I wasn't sure whose they were but I had some anyway. I told her I wasn't that hungry but I had to keep my tummy quiet. That was a lie, of course, but I couldn't let Sekhmet know that I stole some of those biscuits, she might have had a bad opinion of me.

She smiled and told me the biscuits were there for me, that this was *the* place and that, from now on, everything would be fine for me. Oooohhhhhhhh, so the biscuits, they were for me? I felt less guilty then. How very nice, left for me, very charming indeed. I was lost in my thoughts of biscuits and a good night's sleep on a clean bed and, before I knew it,

Sekhmet was kissing me on my pink nose once more! I was stunned, I was not expecting a kiss. She told me not to worry, I would see my new friends very soon. She made a move towards the window.

"Oi, where are you going? Come back here!"

She looked at me as if to say, "Is this any way to talk to a lady?" So I re-phrased to, "Come back here, please."

Sekhmet came back and asked, "What do you want now?"

"Well," I said, "where are you going? You're not going to leave me here alone, are you?"

"You won't be alone," she said.

"But, heck, there's no one here, no one to talk to."
"Your new friends will be coming soon."

"When?"

"Soon."

"I can't see anyone, I don't want to stay here!"

"Be quiet, they'll be coming soon."

"Never mind about the others, where are you going?"

"To do my duty."

"Duty, what duty?"

"My duty is where I'm needed".

"Never mind about where you're needed, I need you here. I don't want you to go, I'm all alone here, we need to talk, to talk a lot, wait a minute." That's all well and good, and easy to say but I'm the one who's here, using his arms to move around and with no one to talk to, so no way could she go, she was going to have to stay and keep me company, no way would I let her go! While all this was going on, spinning around my mind, Sekhmet was looking at me smiling. I was in such a state. I told her, "Never mind smiling, I don't want you to go!" Simple as that! For the first time in my entire very small life I felt so bossy talking to her in such a fashion but I had no choice; if I didn't make my point she'd go again leaving me all alone with no one to talk to.

Sekhmet just had time to repeat that I shouldn't worry, that from now on my new friends would take care of me, when we heard some noise, ooooooooohhhhhhhh, noise. And that was no longer my tummy rumbling! Some real noise.

Sekhmet told me she needed to go. And off she went through the window.

My letter is getting long, so I'm going to take a break right now.

Best wishes, more later,
Norman

4. Now, the friends

Good afternoon,

How are you now? I had a little nap, now I'm ready to carry on telling you about finding myself at Wild Berry.

When Sekhmet left me, I felt lost, completely lost. What would I do now without her? Why had all this happened to me? Why was I in such a nice place without her? What was the point? I couldn't see the elves now. I was ready to curl up, and wanted to go to sleep, maybe for ever. But, before I had the time to finish thinking what I was thinking, the noise became louder. I didn't know what to expect; what could it be? And Sekhmet wasn't even there to protect me.

What is it, I thought. Who is it? Maybe it's someone coming for the biscuits; I'm in so much trouble, I'm going to be in real trouble. Wait a minute, Sekhmet told me the biscuits were there for me, right?

I was in a state, who could it be?

Blissssssssssssss.

Two ladies, not one!

Two?? Two.

OOOOOHHHHHHHH, HOLY MACKEREL!

Two ladies.

One had the voice of an angel. She wasn't talking, she was singing a melody. She was the sort of lady that you would tell the most precious secret to. The sort of lady that makes you want to jump up into her arms and curl up around her neck. The sort of lady that makes you think, as long as she's around, nothing bad could ever happen.

I stretched my neck to see what and who it was, I couldn't wait to see. I stretched again, I'm so tiny, I wished I was taller. I stretched a bit more, and she came into view. Just as I said, I wanted to jump up around her neck. But all I could do was look at her. What a voice; I'd have no more worries as long as she was around. Well, as a matter of fact, I thought it was Sekhmet, transformed into a person. I'll never have any more worries, no one will ever harm me, I thought, as long as she is around. Later on I learned that she was called Val.

I told you there were two ladies, not one, right?

The second one was going around and around. I couldn't wait to see her but I'm so tiny that I couldn't reach up to see her at all. Her voice was also very nice and I thought to myself, as long as she's around too, I'll be all right. I was stretching and stretching and doing my best to see her but I'm so small that I just couldn't quite do it.

This was a lot of stress for someone like me; all these changes, a beautiful new place. Ooooooooohhhhhhhhh, it was so tiring, very tiring. I knew now that Val was around and nothing could ever happen to me, so I allowed myself to go to sleep for a while. I just had no strength left to see who the second lady was, it just had to wait for later on. It was just bliss to go to sleep then. I had that little voice inside me tell ing me not to worry and I knew that Val was there, she was there for me. For the first time I slept deeply, very deep and I slept a long time.

Voices woke me up, nice voices. Very nice voices, they sounded just like fairy voices. Whose are they, I wondered. It's OK, it was Val, she was very busy with what she was doing, she was coming and going, it was just nice to hear her voice. But who was the second voice? Up to that time I had been unable to put a face to that voice and I kept wondering, who is she? Oh, well, I'll soon find out, I thought, and if I don't, I'll ask Val, she'll tell me, I'm sure.

All of a sudden, I turned around, and oh dear, oh dear, what a beauty! Standing in front of me was the most beautiful creature on earth! Even more beautiful than Sekhmet; now that was an achievement, how could that possibly be? How could there be anyone on earth prettier than Sekhmet? Her skin was as white and creamy as milk, her hair seemed to be borrowed from the coat that Sekhmet gave me, all black and shiny. Her eyes were like a hundred carats of pure precious stones, the purest of purest emerald that one can find – a beauty on earth, boy, was she beautiful! Oh, that was an understatement. Her smile was bliss, she didn't need to talk at all, those eyes and that smile were doing it all for her.

For the very first time in my life, listen to this, for the very first time in my life, I didn't know what to say! Can you believe that? Speechless, that's what I was, just speechless, truly, honest. Those eyes, I was in love, I was, truly!

I was in that state of pure bliss for quite a while. It was like sleeping with my eyes wide open, I'd never experienced such a feeling. I thought I was blessed already when I met Val. I heard later that day that this second lady was called Melissa.

Val and Melissa.

Melissa and Val.

It just felt like Sekhmet had blossomed into two creatures even more lovely than herself. How could that be? How could such a lovely thing happen to someone like me? What did I do to deserve it?

Surely I was the wrong small person? Such a day, so many things happening in one day! Was I dreaming, was all this true? There were so many things going round in my mind. Every time I recall that day, it's like reliving a dream. Even now, writing about it makes me dream.

More soon.

Lots of best thoughts,
Norman

5. And more friends

Hello,

It's me again, with a little more of my story.

I was telling you about Val and Melissa that I'd just met. Not only was I in a really nice place but I was getting fed as well.

Are you sure? Oh, well, if you insist, I'll have some more.

That was Val giving me more biscuits! Could it be that now food would be supplied? And I wouldn't have to bother to get my own?

I was thinking and thinking about what Sekhmet told me during our encounters and I felt like I was dreaming. I was in this place, protected, looked after. I thought it couldn't get any better. I thought, Val and Melissa, this is as good as it gets.

Wrong!

Out of nowhere someone else turned up! I was thrilled to bits. I had only one thought in my head: so many people to talk to now!

But who is this one now? And that's a funny accent, isn't it? Ooohhhh, here he comes. "He." Have I said "he"? This one had such a sweet accent, and I wondered who he was.

Ooohhhh, here he is. Oh, it's a bloke now. That made me feel better; all these women, I needed a bloke to keep me company. Now he's looking at me in a funny way; gosh, he has a suspicious look, he's looking at me so doubtfully, what have I done? He had such a sweet accent, I wondered where he came from.

He had a witty face, and was always twitching his nose; how funny he was.
Ooohhhh, bless you! He kept on sneezing and, ooohhhh, I could see his eyes were watery. What's the matter man, I wondered, you need a doctor to look after you!

This guy smelled important and yet he was so cool, I couldn't figure out who he was and why he was looking at me so sceptically. He really had a lovely face, just like a good friend, a friend that you could be mates with for life. I liked this guy, I liked him a lot. I didn't know him but I already liked him lots and lots.

I want to keep the suspense going for you, so I'll tell you more in a little while.

Bye for now,
Norman

6. Important decisions

Good morning,

I was in the process of telling you about my new friends; now I had three friends to talk to. Well, at the time, I wasn't doing the talking, they were.

I could see that the three of them were talking together. What's going on, I wondered, what are they talking about? Adult people, they always think they're so important, and it's so annoying when someone as small as me can't hear what they're saying. Hey, you lot, I thought, come closer, will you?

You'll never guess what they were talking about, never ! Jointly, they'd decided to name me Peter Ustinov! Why, one might ask? These people didn't know what was what! It was because of my moustache. Yeah, my moustache. Not my eyebrows, my moustache. Because it was curly! I'm telling you, these people really didn't know what was what.

Oh, then he was talking to the ladies, and they all looked sceptical. Tell me, I thought, what have I done? What? Say that again. I overheard I needed a hip replacement and they were talking about putting me on the NHS waiting list. I thought this place was all-inclusive Gold FURR-A coverage! On the NHS waiting list; my very small person on the NHS list!

Oh, now he was talking with his funny accent, and they were all talking together, and looking at me. I was getting concerned, I couldn't t hear what they were saying and I was thinking, come closer, will you? Oh, that's better! Oh, now they've decided, he's going to do the job himself. What job?

Can't be the Italian Job, this bloke hasn't got the right accent for it! I wonder what he means. Oh, now they're closer, that's better. Aaaahhhhhh, I see! Val's telling him what to do. Typical woman, right? I know now who's the boss here! Poor bloke, really; how can he survive in there with all these women? She's telling him to do my hips! I see, someone has some good sense, at last! Oh, gee, all these people talking about me, I feel so important!

Oh, well, they've reached a consensus they can see it's like the L'Oréal range, "because I'm worth it!"

My hips will be done at Wild Berry, the job will be done by this bloke with a twitchy nose! My operation will be a lengthy and pioneering one, a real work of art in modern engineering and steel design. I was even to be installed in a steel safety belt to protect my hips. This bloke was brilliant you know!

Before I tell you more about it, I need a drink. More later, then.

All the best,
Norman

7. Losing my credit cards, gaining my identity

Hello,

I'm back with my story: I was telling you about my big operation. While I was being pampered and looked after (I'm glad I could benefit from the Gold FURR-A coverage after all, all-inclusive; it was a real four-star-plus treatment), this guy had another brilliant idea. You'll never guess what that was. No, no, no, not that, not that!

Guess what he did? Go on. Go on, have a guess. He cut my credit cards off. Yep, he jolly well did! I can't believe it either! I had little say in the matter, he did it all by himself. I went to sleep one minute and the next thing I knew my credentials were no longer there!

I have forgiven him, though, I'm quieter now! Which is not such a bad thing for the sanity of the people who'll look after me in my future life!

Ooohhhhh, forgot to tell you something important! Guess what?! My vibrissae dropped. Yeah, truly, honest. What? You don't know what vibrissae are? Now really, how could you not know? Think harder! No, not that, I already told you before that my credentials were chopped off. My vibrissae, my moustache! Yeah, they dropped, no longer styled à la Ustinov.

That was all I needed! So now they've decided to call me Norman instead! Yeah, this is why my name is Norman. Humans! They don't know what they want, do they?! From Peter Ustinov to Norman. So, you've guessed by now, right? Try a bit harder. In ancient times I was worshipped. OK, you've got it. YES, I'm a cat! A black and white cat, with green eyes! The guy with a funny accent is my best mate, I owe him my life. He is called Nico. He's my vet, the best vet on the entire planet. I can now walk again, thanks to Nico.

I walk. I jump. I climb. I'm a very, very happy cat!

Since I was found by Sekhmet and her elves and then looked after at Wild Berry, I promised myself that I would keep a diary. Yeah, truly, a diary; I can write too you know! I want to keep a diary so that I can write down everything that happens to me. I want to talk and write and never stop doing so for the rest of my life!

More later then, all the best,
Norman

8. My education at Wild Berry

Dear All,

Now that you know Nico performed that engineering architectural work on me, I'd better let you know what happened next, right?

For eight long weeks after the operation I had to be kept in a confined space at Wild Berry so that not only could I learn how to behave in society, but also so that I could get lots of physiotherapy for my legs.

Melissa took care of my physiotherapy; it was such long and tiring work. I had to learn to walk all over again. Oh yeah, I forgot to tell you, my pelvis was broken in four places and my hips were totally separated from my spine; you're impressed, right? Yeah, I knew that if I told you, you'd be impressed. So now you know why I had to learn to walk all over again. Beautiful Melissa had a lot of patience with me, she did so much for me. It was lots of fun too because at weekends she took me home with her, so I had my little outings and could play with some friends at Melissa's.

As far as my education about how to behave in society was concerned, they all had a go at it. It was even harder work than the physiotherapy! One was telling me this, the other was telling me that, and you shouldn't do this, you shouldn't do that, little cats don't do this but do that instead. Dearie, dearie me, so much to learn all in one go, I can tell you!

Initially I couldn't use my right leg much. For some reason, I used my knuckle instead of putting my foot flat, but I was

33

getting back into good health and shape. Sooooooo, then came the time when it had to be decided which human family I'd go to live with! That's another story!

I'd learnt by then the secret of charming. As a matter of fact, it was innate so it didn't need too much effort to learn. Also, with the beautiful eyes that I was given by Sekhmet, I didn't need to make much effort to be charming. It just turned out that everyone wanted to adopt me ! It made my ego get ever so big!

Everyone wanted me to go and live with them but, one had four cats already, one had dogs living in the house and I don't like dogs that much, one had yet another problem, so no one knew for sure what my next address would be. In the meantime my address remained Wild Berry!

More later! And all the best,
Norman

9. Does one buy Pee-Dee-Gree at Argos too?

Hello everybody,

Gosh, they were so busy at Wild Berry! Four-legged creatures coming and going all the time, some very posh, some with Pee-Dee-Gree, whatever that means. I don't really know but it sounds impressive. (I wonder if it's a disease.) Some working creatures, some others good enough to eat!

Geeeeeeee, the ones with that Pee-Dee-Gree thing (I was told it's a very important title), they have funny names, right? All double-barrelled names. Gordon Bennett, do they take themselves seriously! Not only are they born with this Pee-Dee-Gree burden, poor souls, but they're also born with a superiority complex. Have you seen them? Gosh, they look down on you as if they were royalty. And their names, I can't get over some of the names I heard, I tell you. And all they could come up with for me was Norman!

I saw so many creatures with this Pee-Dee-Gree thing, I ended up being so impressed by them, it got me thinking, and one day I told myself that maybe I could bribe someone and get some for myself! Maybe I could find another cat or a dog that had too much of it and wouldn't mind giving me some. Maybe I wouldn't even need to use bribes, just maybe! I really thought that if I could call myself Norman Pee-Dee-Gree, I would be important too, right? I tried hard, very hard!

One day a very posh cat turned up. All sleek, his coat was a very light colour, he'd got brown ears and blue eyes. I thought to myself, gosh, that one looks expensive. And I also thought, this kid must be loaded with this Pee-Dee-Gree thing, for sure he must be, so I said to myself that I'd swallow my pride and ask this kid for some.

"Hey, you. Yeah, you there. Do you have some Pee-Dee-Gree to spare? I could do with some." The look I got! Do you think he said a word?! He just looked at me as if I was nuts. I thought maybe he didn't understand my question or maybe, you know, his ears hadn't been cleaned properly. So I asked again, "Can you spare some Pee-Dee-Gree, please? I can let you have some of my biscuits." The only thing he did was to look at me again and then turned his back on me! Truly, what kind of manners is that? I said, "Well, if that's the way one gets with this Pee-Dee-Gree infection, then I'd rather stay as I am." Don't you agree with me?

On another occasion there was another kid with too much of that Pee-Dee-Gree doodah. I think he was called a Persian of some sort. The poor soul, I wonder if his mum combs him? Man, his fur was all over the place, I wonder what he looks like first thing in the morning. His face was so flat, the poor thing couldn't breathe! Never seen such a thing, I wondered how he got such a flat face. I tried to push my nose against the wall several times to see if I could flatten my face too. I was still after this Pee-Dee-Gree thing and I thought, if I can get a flatter face, maybe someone will recognise that I deserve some of this stuff. I pushed and pushed my nose against the wall but to no avail. I asked this kid, I said "How on earth did you get this face? It looks to me as if your mum starved you for weeks and then someone drew a good steak on a wall and let you loose. You wanted to get this steak so you jumped at the wall with your nose first! SLAMMMMM! You did your nose! Is that what happened?! Just tell me if they starve you, and don't go back with them, I'll keep you here with me, man.

36

I'll ask Val to give us enough biscuits for two, no worries, mate. Don't go back if they starve you, you've got such a face mate!"

I felt so sorry and worried for this poor kid. All he could do was lick his nose. Gosh, every time he tried, his tongue reached his eyes, going over his nose. Gee, that was scary, scared me off completely. He tried to mumble some words but his voice was so thick, he sounded like he had all his tubes full of rotten cold, poor thing. He put me right off that Pee-Dee-Gree thing, I can tell you.

So as you can see, I tried hard to get a little of that Pee-Dee-Gree but these two episodes put me right off the stuff; too much hassle. One thing I noticed with these posh kids; you know, they might look and behave like royalty, and were treated like royalty too, but have you seen their baskets? I bet you didn't notice, right? Go on, have a go. Oh, go on, try harder. The thing is, they might all be super posh and have those double-barrelled names but their baskets are still bought at Argos like everybody else's!! Yeah, they have these cheap-looking baskets from a street shop! So what's the point of having Pee-Dee-Gree?

That's when I finally told myself, boy, all this hassle, maybe a flat face and a plastic basket from a common shop? No way, my boy, you ain't gonna pursue this thing! I'm sure you agree with me here, so I'll love you and leave you. I need a little nap and will tell you more later.

Bye for now,
Norman

10. How I met my new mum and dad

Good morning,

Coming back to talking about the place where I'd be moving to, one day a lady came to Wild Berry with a really good-looking sheila, black and white too. Geeeee, she was pretty. The four-legged one, I mean, the other one was too old for me. After this black and white sheila was looked after, Melissa asked the lady whether she wanted to adopt a little four-legged boy, called Norman. The lady was tempted, but permission needed to be obtained from Him Indoors.

"There's no way, it's out of the question." God had spoken, that was his answer.

Oh, well, it was worth trying.

Nothing else was ever mentioned again.

But, guess what. Go on, have a guess. Nothing was mentioned all right, but that wasn't to say that Sekhmet and her elves had nothing to say. Yep, they're still around! Anyway Sekhmet whispered a few words into that lady's husband's ear, and the elves told him, "You'd better do as you're told, matey."

So, now then, it's a bit complicated but I'll try to explain it to you in simple words. Him Indoors, as he was called, he got in touch with Melissa and told her that he would allow me to go and live with them, but it couldn't be for another two weeks. Why? Because he wanted to give the lady a present. A present, because it was her birthday! Yes, in two weeks' time. So he thought he'd get away with murder this year, she'd get a cat for a present! Melissa took care of me for the two extra weeks. I was pampered like mad. I went to her house again and could play with her four-legged family.

Oohh, and guess what. I got to meet one of Melissa's little boys, he's from the ginger brigade and, just like me, he'd had a bit of a difficult time with his legs some months ago. Nico performed one of his engineering works of art on him too and guess what, it's so funny, but his plumbing doesn't work too well. No, not Nico's, you dope; the cat's plumbing. He has to wear Pampers. Honest! Every night Melissa puts on his Pampers so that he can live a comfortable life, and this little chap is so happy!

So now, back to these people I'm supposed to go and live with. The date of her birthday approached, it was on the Monday. It had been a very tough week, with one thing and another, things were not that bright between them two, but I won't go into details. Good job the elves were there.

Anyway, on the Saturday before the Monday (are you with me?), she thought she'd do her shopping as usual, she'd thought she'd go alone, just to have some peace and quiet. But Him Indoors told her, "I'll come with you."
"Oooooooohhhhh," she said, well, I can't really repeat what she said. So off they went, as usual, she wanted to go one way, he went the other; typical.

To keep the peace she bit her tongue and said nothing. Well, nothing for half a second, then she asked, "Where are we going?" Him Indoors told her they were going for a ride. Guess where they ended up. You got it, at Wild Berry!

Melissa and my new dad had organised everything and kept it secret between the two of them for all this time! My new mum was so moved, she didn't know what to say. I told you all along that these little elves can pull so many neat tricks.

Before I could go with them to my new home, they had to wait for Nico to be free. No way they'd let me go just like that. Nico explained this and that and what I should do, and more importantly, what I should NOT do. I already had other ideas in mind.

I left Wild Berry with mixed feelings. On the one paw, I was sad leaving. It had been such a safe place and I was used to everyone there. On the other paw, I was happy to go to a proper home where maybe I would have some brothers or sisters to play with, but mostly that I could talk to.

I left Wild Berry but I promised Nico that I would write, yeah, write to him, write to him every week. Yep, truly, write to him every week, to let him know what was happening to me and how things were going on around me.

I'm going now, I'll write soon, I promise.

Love from
Norman

11. How I became knighted

Hello all,

Norman. Yep, that was my name. My new mum didn't like it, didn't like it at all! What could I do? She just didn't like it. I could hear her and my dad talking about my name, and about some alternative names.

Guess why my new mum didn't like my name. Humans have complicated minds. OK, I know, I admit, at Wild Berry they could have used a little more imagination and found me a better name than Norman. My new mum didn't like my name because one of my new dad's colleagues was called Norman. He was a little bit on the posh side, a highly educated scientist, a good man, one who commands respect on first sight and my mum thought that all it needed was for this guy to turn up at the house and find out that his name had been given to a four-legged creature. Geeeeee, that would have created a diplomatic incident, right?

One point that worried my mum and dad in changing my name was the fact that there were already two black and white four-legged sheilas in the house. I told you about the pretty one already. They were worried that if for any unforeseeable reason I wasn't happy with them and they had to return me to Wild Berry, I would get all confused with a new name, new house, new people, new siblings and then back to square one. They simply thought it wasn't right.

So they thought, oh well, Norman it is. On the table, however, there was a book, a history book, a very old book. To this day

I'm certain that Sekhmet intervened out of the blue and put it there, believe me! Either Sekhmet or the elves! Listen to what happened. This book was on the coffee table and it was so intriguing. I had just arrived here so I hadn't had time to sit down and read it but, right from the very first day I got here, I often sat on top of it. I had no idea what the book was about at first, but it was magic just looking at the cover. It was dark red and green leather with gold letters, a very thick book. I felt like I wanted to step into its magical pages and walk off into history. Yes, that was exactly how I felt, just looking at it. I learnt later that it's written in Italian, but did that really matter? No, on the contrary, I'd say it only added to the magic; a language I couldn't understand would let my imagination run even wilder. I felt like I was turning the pages.

Once into this magic book I could see old castles set in magnificent countryside, hills with deer running free and knights on horses, beautifully adorned with coats of arms and heraldry in gold, reds, blues, greens, gold again. There were beautiful ladies dressed in magnificent long dresses waving to their knights with coloured handkerchiefs, trumpets ringing out household announcements, a cavalcade in the fields below the castle, the drawbridge being pulled down.

Ooohhhh, I open my eyes. Open my eyes? What happened? Was I dreaming? I think I was. I found myself stretching. Had I been sleeping? I'm confused, was I sleeping, or wasn't I?

All of a sudden I heard my dad shouting. Gee, my dad shouting could wake an entire army immediately! My dad had this brilliant idea, yes, yes, listen to this. I heard my dad say to mum, "Let's call him Sir Norman." That was it. Sir Norman I became! I was knighted! I wasn't dreaming after all, now they call me *Sir Norman*. I felt so very important, now I was called Sir Norman, no need for that Pee-Dee-Gree stuff, I was Sir Norman, I'd been knighted by the king of hearts, my dad!

One of the funniest things about ending up with this mum and dad is that to this day I wonder why so much time was spent on my education and manners. My dad's Australian and my mum's Italian, so what was the use of learning all these good manners, I ask you? I could have done without all the fuss, what's the point? And when I think how funny I thought Nico's accent was, you should hear my mum and dad. Sometimes I get the feeling that if I learned Japanese I'd understand them better, geesh, I tell you!

The two four-legged sheilas I was telling you about, they were black and white just like me! The very pretty one is called Black Gold, she's very pretty, very, very. She's posh, she poses; at times they call her Princess Black Gold, and that says it all. The other one is called Pirate. They are twin sisters! Pirate is bigger. Gee, she scares me! She's a big girl.

You know what? You'd swear that we're all from the same family, as our coats are so very similar. It's weird, even our markings are very similar. I'm sure Sekhmet and the elves visited my new sisters too some time ago. We'll see.

I've got to go now,
lots of love,
Sir Norman

12. My first letter from home

Dear All at Wild Berry,

I thought I'd drop you a line instead of phoning so that you'll all know about my weekend here. As you know, I was collected on Saturday morning and my drive to my new home was without incident. My new dad was quite happy because at long last he managed to keep my new mum quiet; it was such a shock to her, the way it all happened on Saturday morning.

When I arrived at my new home, as you can expect I was a little lost, shy and intimidated, so I selected my new residence behind the sofa (it was my own little way of organising a confined space so that I could feel safer). I can't recall how many times they tried to pull the sofa and move it so that I'd come out from behind there. I just didn't want to know. Eventually they adjusted to my way of living and out came the water bowl, the litter tray and food dishes in the front room. I was also given a wicker basket with a nice cover but I wasn't in a mood to like it. I sulked for a couple of hours behind the sofa.

Eventually, by late afternoon I ventured out under the dinner table. Black Gold came to introduce herself. We rubbed noses, and we kissed a bit. I thought I was on to a good thing on my first outing! All of a sudden she swore and spat at me like hell. I was lost for words and my new dad told me, "Don't try to understand a woman, mate." She disappeared upstairs for the rest of the evening, and I went back to sulking behind the sofa. On Saturday evening I started to explore the room. I was intrigued by everything and I adore the plants they have here;

one little palm is just about high enough for me to play with the leaves. They also thought I was mute, but when I came out that night I had a full conversation with my dad. I'm not sure I was that happy so I was walking around moaning and really not convinced that I should be here.

I discovered that the second creature living here (they call her Pirate) behaves like a Queen Bee! Anyway, while I walked around the room moaning, the Queen Bee was under the dining table looking at me, she was lying there like an Egyptian cat (talk about posing). I was still going around moaning. All of a sudden, without any warning, she spat at me like a tiger! She scared the living daylights out of me and I jumped backwards. I sought refuge behind a huge pot plant and looked at her from behind it for the rest of the evening. Everybody was so amused, I wondered if she really meant such serious business! My dad told me that Pirate has a very special routine at night; she gets cuddles from him on the sofa and then she goes to sleep. My moaning and wandering around prevented her doing so and NO ONE disturbs Pirate's routine. I told you she's more like a Queen Bee.

I got them worried for two reasons: (1) I didn't want to eat anything and (2) I like climbing. Did you know that? They stayed up quite late to keep me company and I found it so amusing to climb from behind the sofa or the armchair. I made my new mum quite worried because, of course, my back legs can't hold my weight properly and I kept sliding down, landing on my back legs.

I was told they weren't worried about the upholstery but if I didn't stop climbing they'd tie me up. Whether they meant it or not, I'll never know. I wandered out a little more to the corridor and the kitchen and discovered there are stairs. Every time I made a move someone was behind me. I looked at the stairs several times and my mind was telling me, you can make it, but my legs wouldn't follow and every time I looked at the stairs I had someone behind me saying, "Don't even think about it." I strongly felt both mum and dad were reassured that I couldn't go upstairs and I heard my dad saying to mum "There's no way the kid is going to make it upstairs."

I was confined for the night to the front room.
By 3:15am I'd had enough of being alone so I started calling out for some company. When my new mum came down I ate some biscuits and I even agreed to use my wicker basket.

Sunday I got them worried again because I wouldn't come out of my new basket and never ate anything all day. Then I came to life about 8:00pm! I was going around, very chatty and full of energy when everybody was about to go to bed! So they stayed up a little longer. They discovered then that not only do I like climbing but I also made several attempts at jumping onto the coffee table. Couldn't make it though, so my dad emphasised the fact that there was no way I could make the stairs.

Black Gold came down and we kept each other company, albeit with some distance between the two of us, but at least she didn't spit at me like she did the day before.

I was confined again to the front room for the night. My mum left me some biscuits and half a sachet of HiLife tuna and salmon. I started shouting out for some company at 6:00am this morning, which was a considerable improvement on the night before. Mum came down and was full of praise because I ate all my biscuits and the wet food as well, I got so many compliments. Once I was happy that I'd got them up, I went back into my basket!

Mum made the tea and went back up to the bedroom, but she left the front room door open. I could feel the girls were upstairs, Pirate was having a cuddle with her dad. All of a sudden I too appeared upstairs, and started to chat to my dad. You should have seen them with their mouths open! My dad told me I was, "A determined little sod!" Mum carried me back downstairs and dad came down too and so did the girls. I felt so important!

I was very active this morning and it was very evident that my back legs were improving by the hour. Tthey told me that I was walking almost straight, without limping. My dad was quite amazed.

I'm getting pretty impatient because I want to go out. They barricaded the doors so that I can't leave the room but I scratch the floor and try to push the barrier with my head so that I can go out. Mum's worried because Nico said I'm to be confined to one room for a few more weeks yet. And this morning I ended up upstairs. She can't get over it; she said she'll phone you later to see whether I need to be tied up!

I think I like it here, I have such lengthy conversations with my dad. Black Gold was looking for me this morning, and twice mum found her talking to me on the other side of the barrier. All the doors were open this morning and we didn't fight, there was no spat, no swearing. Black Gold's cystitis didn't flare up and she's quite relaxed. Pirate is still keeping her distance, but I was told she'll be OK. I'm strongly considering allowing these people the privilege of looking after me: I shall keep you informed about how things develop.

Lots of love to you all,
Sir Norman

PS: I always keep my promises! I said I'd write, I will do often.

13. My dad

Hello everyone,

I want to tell you all about my dad! At first I was scared of my dad. Funny thing to say but I was! Not him exactly though, it was his voice. He has such a powerful voice. Every time he spoke, I jumped! He scared the living daylights out of me. Every time he spoke I thought he would eat me alive! Truly, I'm only small, and although I talk a lot, he's worse than me.

My dad says that I have the lungs of Pavarotti, because when I decide to shout or call someone, I do so with determination. My dad says that I have such a good voice. He can talk! After a couple of days, though, I got used to my dad's voice, and I wasn't scared of him any more and I'm developing a huge amount of love for him; I'll tell you all about that in a minute.

My dad calls me 'mate'. Which is funny really; if you ever see my dad, he's nothing like me! I'm so tiny and he's got big shoulders and a big belly too. Ooops, careful now, don't go and say he's fat, he gets offended, he says he's got relaxed muscles.

When I get scared, and it does happen now and again, I run towards my dad; I know he'll protect me.

I've got this funny habit. My dad likes snacks and every time he opens a packet of crisps or maize snacks, I always need to have a look to see what it is but I also always put one of my little paws into the bag! I don't eat anything but I need to put my paw into the bag!

My dad is really funny, you know; he's scared to death of my mum! When he's done wrong, he walks around the house talking to himself, saying he's in trouble with the mafia, especially when it comes to one of us.

Listen to this. A few days after I arrived at my new house, mum had to go out for just a while for some shopping. I was having a little bit of a wild time when I first moved in, so they took it in turns to babysit me. I was free to move around and go out to the garden but I always had someone behind me, reminding me they were there, so that I wouldn't get into any trouble, or better said, no unnecessary *additional* trouble. Anyway, my mum told my dad a dozen times she needed to go out and all he could say was, "Yeah, yeah." She told him he needed to keep an eye on me, and again it was, "Yeah, yeah." Eventually she went off. She wasn't gone more than an hour, and when she got back, my dad was in a state, all white and out of breath. He didn't say hello to mum or nothing, all that he could say was, "This babysitting bit's got to stop. This kid is killing me." That was me!

What happened was that because he wasn't paying attention to mum before she went off out, mum never told him where I was hiding so when my dad eventually came out of his study, he went downstairs but couldn't find me. He went to the bottom of the garden and back three times and searched the house several times but couldn't find me. When mum came back, she found dad in a state but SHE knew where I was and found me straight away. I was under the bed, I hadn't moved!

I've been with my new mum and dad for a few days now and already I've caused a little bit of havoc in the house. I was rather concerned that I'd be sent back to Wild Berry in an express pack, marked special delivery, so just in case it happened, I decided to write another note to Nico, you know, just in case, when one's been naughty.

Lots of love,
Sir Norman

14. I have been naughty again

Hello, remember me?

I'm that cute little black and white creature with innocent green eyes and I'm writing to you because I have encountered, and caused, some trouble and I want to tell you all about it.

All day Wednesday my dad couldn't get a connection to his emails on his laptop. On Wednesday night he asked my mum whether she'd used it and if so had she found anything strange with the connection. After checking and double-checking they found out that I'd chewed the connecting cable! My mum had seen me playing with the cable a few times but thought nothing of it. My dad showed mum all the little teeth marks along the cable, and where I put my teeth through it. That was Wednesday.

Yesterday morning my mum saw me looking around in my dad's study. I like hiding between the shelves and seeing if I can play with some of the files that I can reach. After a while my dad started working there but the telephones were playing up. He called BT to have the lines checked. It was clear something wasn't working quite right but, look no further, I'd managed to pull the cables from their sockets.

Today, GEEEEEEEE, I was told off.

I always wake up very early and start the day with a big bang, like a bag of dynamite. At 05:45am, I wanted to surprise them and climb on the bed but it's too high so I couldn't make it but at least after I'd tried I was happy because I'd got everybody up. Everyone was then served breakfast and the house was rather quiet. All of a sudden there was a panic because they couldn't find me. They searched the entire house and my mum was upstairs looking for me. She looked through a top window and much to her horror she saw me. Guess where I was – in next door's garden.

My dad couldn't believe it, my mum was horrified. I just climbed over the fence which isn't too high at the bottom of the garden. You know, they have two dogs next door; doesn't bother me! My dad also climbed into next door's garden. It wasn't even 7am and he was still in his pyjamas, so was mum. I knew by then I was in deep trouble and I panicked a bit so I was running all over their garden and so was dad. Eventually mum got me when I was trying to go over a bigger fence that leads to the fields. When I realised I was back in my own garden, I didn't want to be carried in mum's arms, so she put me on the ground and I ran all the way from the bottom of the garden indoors. My dad thought I was speed-training for the next Olympics!

I ran upstairs to mum's work room and I was so excited about my early morning performance that I wanted to carry on. I managed to climb onto a chair and then onto mum's table. I played football with a few pens, a few CDs and other various things she had there. I got everything on the floor, then I jumped straight from the table to the floor, then I hid under the bed. My dad told me I'd better stay there for the day so that mum could chill off, she was mad at me and mad at my dad because I climbed the fence. So he promised her that this weekend he'd fix it and put up a higher panel or something.

Nico had said, "He'll be OK but he'll never be an athlete." He also said that "His 'credit cards' are off, so he'll be quieter." I climb, I jump, I run, I go next door. My dad says that I'm the happiest little terrorist he knows!

By the way, Black Gold is getting really friendly and Pirate is getting easier on me.

I'll try to behave over this long weekend but I can't promise, I'll just try. Have a good Bank Holiday.

Lots of love from
Sir Norman

P.S: Yep, I tell you, my mum was really mad that day: I don't think it was because she didn't love me, it's just that she was so worried about my legs. One minute they were told by Nico what I should do and specifically what I should NOT do and just a few days later, I go Rambo-ing all over the place; I told you I had ideas of my own!

15. My sisters

Note: As I told you, I've now got two sisters, also black and white but instead of having green eyes as I do, they have golden eyes, yeah, gold, that makes them so posh! They are twins but couldn't be more different in their behaviour and manners. I know that Nico has looked after them for several years now but I bet he's got no idea what goes on in this house with these two, so I decided to let him know the truth.

Hello Nico,

For several years now you've looked after Pirate and Black Gold. For sure they're beautiful, especially Black Gold. But Nico, you've got no idea how they rule the house and how much attention they require. I tell you, they rule this house! Say if you jump on the wrong armchair, for instance, you get told off, they shout at you, swear, spit; you name it, they'll do it, truly.

The Pirate has a funny attitude to life. It's "Been there, done that, got the T-shirt and now I'm completely blasé." She won't take one step more than necessary if she can help it! My dad says she's a very good hunter as long as the birds fly into her path. A few days ago everyone was outside on the patio and Pirate was sitting in the middle of the garden. Some birds flew over low, and only Pirate's eyes moved, watching where these kamikaze birds were heading. Then all of a sudden she just sat up on her back legs and, with the minimum effort, raised her two arms in the air, and guess what. A bird got stuck in her front paws. Truly, no, no, I don't fib, she just did that, raised her arms and bingo! The poor bird, say no more!

Pirate's good though. My mum also calls her either Teddy
Bear or Granny, depending on how much Pirate moans. If
she gets out of bed in the morning on the wrong foot then
for sure my mum calls her Granny. Pirate's also very intelli-
gent; she has different tones of voice and my dad always lis-
tens to what she says. Very often she comes indoors to let him
know either that Black Gold is fighting with an intruder or has
got a bird or whatever. Pirate even comes in to tell my dad it's
raining, so that he can go out and get the cushions back in,
truly, she tells my dad, she's really great.

Pirate's very protective of our sister and my mum said that
she's starting to be protective of me as well. I don't see it
though, not yet. But I heard my mum saying to dad the other
day that two bully toms were walking along the garden wall
while I was on the patio. Clearly they were intrigued because
they'd never seen me before. Well, Pirate was walking beneath
them in the garden so they wouldn't come down, and now
and again she glanced at me, nice old Granny!

Take this morning, for example. Mum and dad were very busy
so I took advantage of that to sneak out. I wanted to explore
the back end of the garden. It's a place that is strictly forbidden to me, again because of the danger to my bad legs. My
mum couldn't find me, so she got her wooden clogs and she
came down the back of the garden, worried about where I
could be. Well, guess what. Pirate was sitting just a few yards
from where I was hiding and as mum went behind the greenhouse and the beans, Pirate was miaowing and looking in my
direction so that mum knew immediately where I was. Pirate
got so much praise this morning and of course I wasn't that
popular! One major funny thing about Pirate is her taste, she
adores westerns! I'm not kidding, she does. My dad's got a

collection of John Wayne videos and Pirate always sits with
dad on the armchair and watches the Indians, the cowboys,
the fights; she always, always watches!

But you'll never guess what Pirate hates. No, you'll never
guess! I've got to tell you. She hates Maria Callas, no joke, she
does! My mum loves opera and she's got some good record-
ings of Callas. No kidding, but if she ever plays Callas, Pirate
leaves the room! Never seen such a temper! Even when
there's opera on the TV, old Pirate's not happy, so the sound
is always turned down; she's a funny old Granny.

As far as Black Gold is concerned, well, you've never seen
such a thing! Nico, do you know how much of a spoilt brat
she is? She was born to be spoilt, I tell you, man! OK, she's
very pretty but does she know it! She walks as if she's an
Egyptian princess, then she poses and looks around her. My
dad always whistles when she passes by because she wiggles
her bum so my dad calls her either Marilyn Monroe or Wiggly
Bum.

Just as well Black Gold never managed to buy herself any of
that Pee-Dee-Gree stuff. Dearie, dearie me, if she'd ever swallowed some, God help us! But guess what I did to her. The
other day she was going past me as she usually does; she walks
by me, gives me a superior look, and then as she carries on
walking, she turns at me and spits, she does it every time. The
other day I'd had just about enough of her insolence so as she
passed by me and spat, I waited for her to walk another step
and then ... wwwwwalllllllllloppppppppppp! I belted her! Truly,
I did. Ooohhhhhh, I'd had enough of her and I belted her on
her back. I jumped a little and then wallopped her a good one!
She was stunned! She didn't know what to say. She never ex-

pected it. Both mum and dad witnessed it and they were so amused. Black Gold wasn't. My dad told me that I was a good lad, standing up for myself. I got so much praise afterwards and Black Gold got a cuddle from mum. Black Gold is lost when mum's not around, it's as if she's glued to mum! Talk about a baby!

She's funny, old Black. One of her favourite places in the house is mum's table in the work room and she spends hours on that table while mum works on her laptop. Black leans on a pile of books at one end of the table and several times I've seen her walking on mum's keyboard; she's quite creative when she walks all over it. Then I've often also seen Black Gold put one of her front paws into mum's hand and then the pair of them sit there, hand in hand. It's cute to see, but I told you she's a mummy's girl.

Sometimes, you go in mum's room and Black Gold is really cute; she always, always sleeps with her head on something. I've seen her sound asleep with her head on one of these huge dictionaries. She could have the leading role in Shakespeare's 'Sound Asleep'.

Anyway, Nico, I just wanted to let you know some of the little secrets of what goes on behind closed doors here.

Keep well, write soon,
Sir Norman

16. My toys

Hello All,

Some more news! When I left Wild Berry, Nico told my mum and dad to make sure they didn't play with me yet or let me play with toys so that there wouldn't be any danger to my legs. But I had totally different ideas. I love my toys. Actually, they're my sisters' toys, but I use them all the same! I love playing, I play for hours on end, I do! There are loads of toys here but my sisters are so blasé about them that they don't use them, so I do and I do it well.

Another of my passions in life is football; I play football with whatever I can! When I left Wild Berry, Val gave my mum a couple of little balls that I played with when I was living at the surgery and I play a lot with them. There are wooden floors here, almost everywhere, so playing football is great.

And there's no carpet on the stairs either. One morning, I was Rambo-ing around a little bit more than usual and my mum was telling me to calm down, but I was having a good game and scoring quite well (my dad said I looked like a little Ronaldo). I was going from one room to another upstairs and then back again but my game was getting a bit routine.

Soooooooo, I decided to spice it up a little bit, I decided to play football on the stairs, polished without carpet, and as if that wasn't enough, I played football going down. Mum couldn't look at me, and dad was laughing! My mum thought she'd find me at the bottom of the stairs, but no way, I wasn't going to give up a good game, and I carried on in the hall and the kitchen. I'm a cat and I was giving my mum kittens; they do say that, don't they?

Lots of love, will write again soon,
Sir Norman

17. Something is parked in the garden

Dear all at Wild Berry,

I wanted to let you know that there's something in the garden.
It looks like a big toy, it's bigger than me, and I can't play football with it. It's been parked there for a few days and I've been
so very intrigued by it. It's red and black and some of the
wires are yellow, if I remember rightly. Oh, and now I come
to think of it, some of the wires are black as well. Every time
my mum saw me roaming around it she'd tell me not to go
too near it as I'd get dirty, and she said it's my dad's toy. It's
got interesting bits on it, plenty of things I've never seen before, several bits and pieces that I'm sure I could play football
with if I could only get hold of them.

My dad can play with it, he's allowed to. I've seen him several
times playing with it, or at least I think he is playing with it; he
can, he's big enough, while I'm only tiny. But humans have
very funny ways of playing. I saw my dad with this thing several times, but he was only turning it around, again and again
and, ooohhhhh dearie me, can he say bad words to it! What's
the point of such a toy if all you can do is swear at it?

One day my dad was playing more than usual with this toy and
a few bits and pieces had come off it and were lying on the
ground. It was still too big to play football with, though, or
throw in the air with my legs. I heard my mum telling dad to
be careful, not to get grease all over himself. My dad was on
his knees, huffing and puffing with this thing. Gosh, if a toy
gives you such a hard time, what's the point of it? I don't understand human beings.

Then, all of a sudden, my dad put all the bits and pieces together again, then I saw him pulling and pulling on a wire. He
was having such a hard time, it seemed to me. Oooohhhh,
every time he pulled that wire, he was saying so many bad
words, my ears curled while I watched all this drama.

Mum came out, she had a word with dad. You know, one of
those words. She told me to go back indoors! Why would I go
back indoors when I was having so much fun watching my
dad? And then, who knows? Maybe at some point I could play
with this toy too, it was big enough for both my dad and me,
why should I go back indoors?

Mum told me I wouldn't like it when it started. Well, by the
look of it and at my dad, it certainly didn't look as if it was
going anywhere, did it? In the meantime, my sisters were
watching from a safe distance; they obviously knew all about it
already.

Meanwhile, my dad was still pulling like crazy on that wire that
wouldn't do anything, whatever it was he wanted it to do. I
was told again to go indoors but didn't listen and dad told my
mum not to worry and that I had to learn sooner or later.

Then suddenly there was an almighty noise. It sounded like,
oh dear, I'd never experienced such a noise before, so I don't
know what it sounded like, such a noise!

I jumped what must have been yards backwards. It scared the
living daylights out of me, dearie, dearie me. And then, as if
the noise wasn't enough, this big toy started moving. I was
some way away by then but seeing this huge toy moving, I
thought if it comes anywhere near me, I'm so tiny, I'll be
swallowed alive. I couldn't comprehend why my mum and dad

were so amused. Then I could see that dad was moving too, pushing this thing in front of him. I didn't know that such a toy existed. Who could possibly have invented such a noisy toy? Can someone tell me?

Eventually I came out of my stupor; it felt for a few seconds as if I'd been glued to the patio. I was so scared I couldn't move, truly, couldn't move at all. When I realised that my dad was moving with the toy, that was it, I rushed indoors like I was running for the Olympics. My sisters watched me whizzing by, then looked at each other. They could've warned me, couldn't they? You tell me, I don't know. I went as far as possible indoors, making sure I was far enough inside to be safe but still near enough that I could see what my dad was doing with that toy. Pirate was not amused by the noise but seemed undeterred by the toy itself. Black Gold, being her usual superior self, remained on her chair but with such a disdainful expression. She was looking at my dad as if to say, "When you've finished with your stupid toy, maybe some other little persons can get some sleep."

Every time dad went further down the garden, I ventured out into the middle of the room where I could see what he was doing but when my dad walked back pushing this horrible thing in front of him, back I went into hiding. What can humans possibly call such a toy?

I was watching Pirate; she didn't seem too bothered. So eventually I emerged a little from hiding. Pirate also had such a disgusted look on her face. I made sure I stayed behind her all the time, I wanted to be sure that if dad came indoors with this thing she'd be in front of me; she's so big I was sure she'd be strong enough to stop this thing. So for the rest of the time that dad was playing with it, I stayed behind Pirate, wondering all the time, how can my dad have fun with his toy just walking up and down the garden pushing it in front of him? One can have fun playing football, throwing things in the air, but walking up and down? That was a funny way of having fun! Can someone explain to me?

That was an experience I'll never forget. That was my first introduction to a lawnmower!

When I have more news I'll write again, much love to you all from Sir Norman

18. In trouble big time – then I made up for it

Good morning all,

It's urgent, this is an urgent message to all of you. I'm writing to you because I got myself into trouble. Yeah, you hear me all right. I've been in trouble, and in trouble big time! I'm writing just in case, so you can take my side, just in case.

You have no idea how much I was told off, you've no idea how much trouble I was in! Even my dad told me off. He was still calling me 'mate', but nevertheless he told me right off, using his 'I-am-not-too-happy-with-you' voice.

The cause of all this trouble is my sister Black Gold. Truly, it's her, not me!

I'm one of the lads, right? I'm just one happy-go-lucky creature, a real bloke. As long as I'm fed, kept clean, not given any hassle, I'm OK. (Well, as far as anything else goes, I can't do much about it; I already told you I lost my credit cards.) So, anyway, I'm a real bloke. I don't like to show off. Well, I tried to get some of that Pee-Dee-Gree stuff but it didn't work, so I just take every day as it comes, and every day brings surprises and excitements aplenty for someone as tiny as me.

Now then, you take Black Gold, she's such a show-off, she behaves like a prima donna. My dad's right, she walks like Marilyn Monroe. She looks down on you, and she always has that look that says "I'm better looking than you." I know that, but she doesn't need to remind me every day, several times a day. Mind you, I have to say, they found a really good name for her, didn't they? Black Gold. I mean, with a name like that, for sure one can expect to be something in this world, don't you think? But, as I told you earlier, it's just as well she never got any of that Pee-Dee-Gree stuff, otherwise, Lord help us, you'd have to get an appointment to speak to her. Though, to be fair, she does wear her name beautifully; she's mostly black and her eyes are gold, so the name Black Gold suits her.

My mum told me that when dad brought Black Gold home some years ago and mum wanted to give her a real good name to give her a better chance in life, so she could start all over again. That's why they called her Black Gold, nothing to do with her colour.

Black Gold and I spend lots of time together, outside in the garden and in mum's work room. Black has two favourite places in this room (I should say had). Mum's table is her favourite place and she spends lots of time there while mum's working. The second place she has/had is a chair covered with one of mum's woolly scarves. It's a really good chair this one; it's comfy, it's warm, it's just big enough for someone tiny. So I nicked it, of course!

Sometimes Black Gold and I play together and we run around the house trying to figure out who's running fastest. When we run up and down the stairs mum always says, "Careful, the cavalry is passing by" or even "Here comes the cavalry".

I must admit that sometimes I annoy Black Gold. She's older than me and wants some peace and quiet and all I want to do is play and go out in the garden. But even so she doesn't need to remind me all the time she's a prima donna.
I've been telling you all this about Black and I realise I haven't

told you yet why I've been in so much trouble. I belted her. I belted her real good! I'd just had enough of her behaving the way she does, I couldn't take much more of her, so I showed her what I'm capable of.

My dad was in the garden with Pirate and me; we were all chatting and having a good time, and mum was in the kitchen. Out of nowhere comes Miss-Princess-I-Am-So-Very-Beautiful and there we go, she walks between my dad and Pirate wiggling her bum, walking slowly so that we all know she's passing by, and looking at us as if we were ordinary people and she was a princess. You know the kind of thing I'm talking about. And off she goes, to attend to her own business. So, as I said, I couldn't take much more of all this rubbish and I wanted to teach her a good lesson, so I jumped on her! Yep, I jumped on her back with my two front legs and all my weight, which isn't all that much yet, but it was enough to scare the living daylights out of her.

The thing is, she wasn't expecting what I did. I don't think I hurt her but because I caught her by surprise she wasn't just really scared, the worst thing is she started screaming, she really screamed! I think that's what made my mum and dad think it was worse than it really was. See, even with this, she couldn't just say a few words to me, just between her and me, oh no, no, no, she has to scream and make a real fuss about nothing. So that I get an ear bashing. And so did dad, actually.

Mum came out of the kitchen like a rocket. "What on earth happened?" Dad said that he just saw me jumping on Black's back. Mum asked who on earth screamed like a 'Cherokee attack on the Confederates?' Gosssshhhhhhh, my dad got a few choice words from mum. I felt sorry for the poor bloke, as it was all my fault to start with. Well, not completely my fault; if only that prima donna had shut up.

Mum asked dad exactly what happened. It felt like he was being questioned in court. (I've seen it on TV, it's impressive.) She was asking questions right, left and centre, trying to find out exactly how, when, and why all this kerfuffle started. Black Gold, now very happy that she'd attracted so much attention, was standing in the midst of us all, grinning like a Cheshire cat. Pirate, true to form, hadn't moved from the chair where she was presiding. She was looking at me and our sister as if to say, "They're only kids."

Anyway, mum started to tell me that I wasn't to behave in such a manner, that I'm not to attack my sister. Geeeeee, I tried to hide behind a tree but it didn't do the trick. My dad told me that I was getting too cocky and that I needed to calm down, then he told me to try and attack Pirate. The man's mad, I'm telling you! Attack Pirate? She scares the life out of me, she's at least five times bigger than me. I took a look at my dad as if to tell him he was mad. My mum told me that this had better not happen again or she would keep me indoors, and she told my dad that if he couldn't keep an eye on us, then he should also remain indoors, poor bloke!

Then, of course, Black Gold had to remind everyone on the scene that she was the centre of attention, so she wiggled her way out of the conference. My mum followed her and told her how very sorry she was, and this and that. And she had to give this pretentious creature a cuddle so that she made her feel even more important than she already thinks she is. While Black was in mum's arms, of course, she has to look down on me, doesn't she? I took one look at her and I whispered, "I

know how to fix this one." I wasn't spoken to for the rest of
the afternoon. And, needless to say, when I spoke, no one
answered me. No one except my dad. That kept reminding
me that both of us were in the doghouse. Again, I said to myself, "I know what to do later."

We were fed and all that stuff without many smiles. My dad
was fed too a little later. Then mum and dad went into the
front room to watch TV and the girls went upstairs. I was
roaming about the room trying to attract as much attention as
I could, throwing my toys in the air, playing football. But
nothing seemed to work with mum, she was really serious. So
I did it. Yep, I did it, I jumped on her lap. I think the old girl
melted! My dad told me that when she's really mad at him, he
brings her flowers. How am I supposed to get her flowers,
then? You tell me! So I said to myself, I'm sure a little cuddle
will do the trick! All of you at Wild Berry, if you hear anything, can you please take my side, not Black's?

Love you all,
Sir Norman

19. The wardrobe

Hello all at Wild Berry,

Just a quick note today to let you know that I won, I won!

I won! I did, seriously. Dad's laughing at mum because I won
the battle of the wardrobe! There's one thing mum's always
been adamant about – the wardrobes. No one's allowed in the
wardrobes. That's a fact, it's as simple as that. The doors of
the wardrobes need to be kept closed at all times, and that's
that.

The girls, who are spoilt, have never been allowed in the wardrobes. Mum always said that we'd leave so much fur all over
the place that it'd be too difficult to clean up after us. Fair
enough. We can't blame her, can we?

But the thing is, I'm fascinated by the wardrobes. I don't
know why, no one knows why.

One day mum was ironing, which means coming and going to
and from different rooms. And I was coming and going with
her, you know, I wanted to keep her company. With all this
coming and going I was talking a lot, really a lot.

My dad came to see what we were doing and asked me why I
was singing as if I were Pavarotti. My dad can't get over the
power of my lungs – he can talk! And while dad was talking to
mum I was shouting even louder to make myself heard. Dad
asked me what I wanted, but all I could do was shout and look
at the wardrobe door, so dad kindly told me that wasn't a

good idea as mum doesn't want anyone in the wardrobes. Nor in any cupboards. I did that in front of several wardrobes and cupboard doors but the one I preferred was my dad's wardrobe. When I was told not to bother, I shouted even louder, still looking at the wardrobe door.

One day, both mum and dad were with me, and all I could do was keep shouting. Dad made a move to open the wardrobe door and mum said to him, "Don't even try." Dad said, "Just let's try to see what he wants."

Of course, as soon as the door was open, I walked in. That was my dad's wardrobe. I made myself comfortable on top of some jumpers folded at the bottom. Mum was really not happy about it but dad tried to convince her that it wouldn't be for long.

I just love the place! Now almost every morning, after my breakfast I take a little nap in my dad's wardrobe. Things have been re-arranged for me to be most comfortable. Mum put dad's jumpers into some baskets so that they stay in a pile, then on top of these jumpers she put an old blanket and on top of the old blanket she put one of dad's old denim jackets, she said that it should protect the clothes from the fur.

It has also been organised for the wardrobe door to remain open, so that I won't be locked in. Dad's laughing at mum for giving in on her wardrobes policy.

Much love,
Sir Norman

20. Pirate educates me

Hello all at Wild Berry,

Do you know Pirate well? I'll tell you about her. Pirate, the Queen Bee, she hasn't got much patience with me! She thinks I'm too much of a bother. I play all the time when all she wants to do is to sleep. And I shout. Well, I wouldn't say that I shout really, I just talk loud or, better still, as my dad says, I have very powerful lungs.

Having said that, she's a good girl, the old Pirate.

Pirate's very funny; she always pretends to sleep when she's out in the garden, most of the time presiding from a chair. But I think she's like a crocodile, you know what I mean? Crocs always pretend to sleep, but their eyes are never completely shut. You can always see them floating on water with just the top of their head poking out, and their golden eyes just about open, you know the sort of stuff. Pirate's just the same, albeit she can't swim like a croc, although she's so big she could float quite well.

Now, you noticed that I said Pirate is 'big' and not 'fat'? My dad gets offended if you say Pirate's fat, and she gets offended too. My dad says she's pleasantly plump, not fat. I'm warning you, never say Pirate is fat, never!

So, I was telling you that Pirate is like a crocodile with her eyes almost shut but not completely. She acts like she doesn't care but she does, the good old Pirate. Dad's seen her several times pretending to sleep but looking in my direction. I might be hiding under a bush but the old girl will be 'asleep' with her head turned in my direction, so even if I'm trying to hide, I'm always found because of this old-crocodile-queen-mother.

Yesterday I was in the garden with Pirate, and she was walking down the garden and I decided to follow her, from a distance I mean. If she ever got a bit annoyed with me and decided to turn on me, Lord help me, she'd flatten me in no time! Now you know why I get on with the old girl, but from a distance!

So she was walking in front of me and I was about three yards behind her. All of a sudden the black tom cat, the real bully that lives at the bottom of the village (despite loving four-legged creatures, my mum always says that this black tom is as nasty and bullying as the family he lives with. My mum feels sorry for him, so do I actually). Anyway, this black tom was walking along the top of the fence, trying to get to the bottom of our garden so that he could get into the farmer's fields beyond. Pirate doesn't like this cat, nor does Black Gold as a matter of fact, they're always chasing him away. My dad was watching all this and he saw Pirate looking at me and while she was turned towards me she made a sound a bit like she was swearing at me, but she wasn't, she was telling me to follow her. Pirate ran alongside the fence where this poor black tom was walking and as she was running down, she was looking back to see if I was following her, which I was. Pirate was making all sorts of noises to scare the black tom off, poor soul really! I was following her all the time, running along and looking up at the fence.

This poor black tom is used to Pirate; he moved to the village a couple of years ago, so he's known Pirate and Black all the time he's been living here. But you know what? He's really scared of this old crocodile!! I mean, for sure, if she got hold of him him, he'd be finished, truly, she must be six to seven times bigger than him. But it's not just that; she doesn't allow anybody in her garden, so that gives her even more strength. When Pirate's annoyed with intruders, she's like a steamroller. That's what dad calls her, a steamroller; she doesn't want anything in her way and she runs towards her target like a rocket, albeit a very big rocket.

Dad said the pair of us were a sight to see.

Now that I could see that Pirate was taking me on a little more, I wanted to impress her. You know, I'm a bloke, she's my sister but I wanted to impress her just the same. I wanted to get some good brownie points with my old sis so I thought if I could only jump up on that fence and chase that black tom, the old girl would be really impressed. And she'd be really proud of her little brother.

So I tried.

Well, sort of.

I'm getting much better every day but my back legs are not quite up to what they should be, it's still early days. I knew I couldn't jump up onto the fence and reach the top and run after that tom, so I compromised. At one point in the garden, leaning on the fence, there's the trunk of an old tree that died off years ago but is still there, so I thought, I'll use this old trunk as a trampoline to jump up on the fence. In my mind I had it all planned.

So I did. Well, again, sort of.

I'm only tiny but, as I jumped on the trunk, it was so old and fragile that I slid backwards all the way down, and fell on the floor on my back, flat as a pancake. Dad, who was still watching the whole thing, rushed over to see if I was OK (he's so scared of mum – chicken!!) but as he was coming towards me, I got myself together and walked straight in front of him as if nothing had happened.

Needless to say, I really didn't manage to impress Pirate. Rather, on the contrary, she was sitting near the greenhouse, watching all the events unfolding in front of her and she took one look at me, a look that was saying something like, "What on earth are you trying to do, you silly kid?" I felt a bit silly for a couple of minutes and kept a low profile for a few hours. I'd so much wanted to impress sis Pirate, but plan A didn't work out.

However, there's always a plan B in life. A few hours after all this happened, there he was again, this black tom, back on the fence. I couldn't believe it! Hadn't he understood that he's not welcome here? I'm telling you, some people are so thick. I couldn't believe that after all that song and dance from Pirate and me earlier this afternoon, this thickhead was back again!

So I thought, here's my chance to impress them all. I failed the first time round, let's have another go at it.
There he was going down the garden, and it gave me great pleasure to run from the middle of the garden towards the fence as if I were a little lion. I rushed full pelt towards the fence and as he saw me coming the black tom made a run for his life. Just as well, because as I reached the fence I had to stop because my back legs won't allow me to climb up a fence. I would've looked ridiculous. Good job I scared the black

tom, and good job he never realised that I could only run, not jump up onto the fence.

Dad called my mum and she watched me chasing the black cat. I got so much praise, my back was patted so many times. It feels so good to be important when you're only tiny! Pirate was presiding from her beloved garden chair and she gave me a nonchalant look. But I'm convinced she was impressed by my actions, she must have been, I don't doubt it.

My dad told me I was a good lad. Pirate heard him saying that, so she turned her back! Typical woman, they can never say anything straight, they'll always pretend not to care. That's what my dad told me, anyway.

Will write more soon.

Much love,
Sir Norman

21. My own independence

Hello Nico, Val and Melissa,

I hope my note finds you well. Just wanted to let you know that I discovered my very own independence. I'm going to tell you all about it.

When I first came to this house, I had a good look around at everything. I noticed a few suspicious things here and there. One in particular was the kitchen door. I was most intrigued by the kitchen door.

When I came here, it was summer and rather a hot summer, therefore all the doors were kept open during the day. Then later on it was still summer but, being England, it wasn't so hot any longer, typical British weather, so the doors weren't open for so long in the evening.

I could never figure out why on earth the kitchen door wasn't finished. I thought the builders hadn't had enough time to finish the door. I also believed maybe mum and dad never had enough money to pay for an entire door so they were given an unfinished door. Maybe that was the explanation for the door with a hole in the bottom. Nevertheless, I could see my sisters finding this quite useful. I saw my sisters going through the door instead of opening the door. That made me also think, geeeee, my sisters are rather lazy, they can't open the door themselves, so they just jump through it!

Both my mum and dad tried several times to teach me to go through this door but I just couldn't comprehend why, on the one paw, they adopted me and let me come to live in their house with them and then, on the other paw, they threw me out of the door without even opening it for me, just throwing me through it. That door really intrigued me. Then several times, I saw my sisters going through it, in and out and I thought to myself, there must be an explanation for this door, for sure there must be.

One particular evening, my mum spent lots of time with me going through this door from the kitchen to outside. Then she was going around to the front room and out into the garden to teach me how to come through from outside to indoors. Thinking back, we went through this little exercise so many times that evening, my mum must have been completely exhausted.

I thought it was a game, like playing football. I thought, maybe going in and out through the door is a game, a pretty boring one, mind you, but a game nevertheless. I thought, this must be a game invented by a very boring human being. I couldn't believe anyone would invent such a stupid game.

I stopped and watched my sisters going through this hole in the door a few more times. Then I tried it myself. I went out first, then I stood in front of the sliding doors to the front room and I was shouting for my dad to open the doors so I could come back in! They were so patient with me that evening. Then I tried it again. Out. And back in. That was my first experience with a cat flap.

Much love from
Sir Norman

22. My auntie Doris

Dear All,

I've got to tell you about my new aunt, she's called Auntie Doris. To say that Auntie Doris is really nice is an understatement. Really, truly, she is the nicest lady you could ever meet and I wanted to tell you what she did for me.

When I got home from Wild Berry, my mum called Auntie Doris to let her know that now Pirate and Black Gold had a little brother. Mum wanted to let her know because Auntie Doris looks after the girls when mum and dad are away; she loves Pi and Black as if they were hers.

Auntie Doris loves four-legged creatures, all of them, she really does. She worries so much about all of them, she can't help it! She does so much work for animal rescue centres, she does charity work and most of all she knits a lot; mum said she must have knitted millions of little blankets already.

When mum called Auntie Doris, she came to meet me immediately. You should have seen the look in her eyes when she first saw me walking with my wobbly back legs. She looked at me then at my mum, then looked at me again and her face was full of worry. I bet her first thought was, "What am I going to do with this little one when I'm asked to look after them?" I'm sure that was what she was thinking.

She went home but after just a little while she came back, bringing me a little blanket, all for me alone, I didn't have to share it with anyone, it was all mine. Mum put the blanket on

the cushion of an armchair and she hasn't been able to remove it ever since! I like it very much, and I'm very proud
of it.

Speak to you soon,
Sir Norman

23. John Wayne on patrol

Dear everyone at Wild Berry,

I've got to tell you something really funny, it's about my dad
and me. In one of my previous letters I told you that my dad
has a passion in life; it's western movies. Not all of them
though, he particularly likes the golden oldies with old actors,
and most particularly he likes cowboys. Now, my dad says of
me that I take my role so seriously in defending my territory
that I look like that John Wayne. It's because my front legs are
slightly bent just like a cowboy's and also because my dad says
that when I walk, it looks like I'm on a mission all the time or
on patrol.

The other day, both my sisters were sitting on the garden
chairs. They usually take it in turns to walk around the garden
and make sure that everything's in good order. So I told them
that I'd like my share of the responsibilities and that from
now on I would patrol the garden too. I know I'm tiny but
I'm getting stronger and stronger by the day so if there were
to be any intruder I could chase him off quite easily.

Pirate looked at me with a suspicious look but she didn't move
from her chair. That was a clear sign to me that I could go
ahead. Sooooo, off I went all by myself patrolling the garden,
all behind my dad's bean plantation, behind the greenhouse,
on one side, on the other side, under the trees, under the
bushes. I wasn't aware of it but my dad was keeping an eye on
me all the time to see where I was and what I was doing and
when I was on my way back to the house my dad could see
me with my little bent front legs and again he called me 'John

Wayne'! That'll be the day! I'm so proud to be compared to that great actor, it makes my day. Looks like I can defend my sisters now without fear from any intruder. My dad's so amused!

I'll see you at Rio Grande!
Sir Norman

24. I don't like that style

Dear all at Wild Berry,

Oh dear, I think I did something else that on second thoughts I really shouldn't have.

Over the past few days, I don't know what's going on but my dad isn't around and my mum isn't in her best mood.

Because my dad isn't around Pirate is really, seriously in a bad mood too. She talks even less than on a normal day, and she doesn't talk to me then anyway. If I talk to her she swears at me real bad, and if I try to go near her in the garden, she walks off to remote corners of the garden where I'm strictly forbidden to go. Gee, I learnt my lesson, talk about being grumpy. All day long she's in a terrible mood! I even heard my mum telling one of her friends that Pirate doesn't eat properly because she misses dad. Mind you, if anyone asks for my opinion, I'd say she could survive quite a few days without food, she's that big! I'll never say Pirate is fat though, all right?

As far as Black Gold is concerned, she behaves like a lost soul. On a normal day she's always glued to mum but these last few days she's always behind mum, she moans at everything, she always wants to be picked up by mum; she must be missing dad as well in her own way. She's more of a friend than Pirate because we play quite a bit together; we love rushing around the house like mad. I told you, mum says "Here comes the cavalry." We run all over the place but when she's had enough of playing she just jumps on mum's table and then she spits at me from the top of the table because I'm not allowed on it!

Can't win them all, can I? I miss my dad too because it's good to have another bloke in the house with all these women. And when dad's not around no one calls me 'mate'. But I don't know where he is and I've still got so many things to learn and explore that I haven't got time to worry about where dad might be. It's as simple as that, I'm too busy, there just aren't enough hours in the day. And very often, not even during the night either.

Tonight my mum left us all on our own for a few hours while she went out. Because of my sisters being in a bit of a funny mood these days, I have to entertain myself most of the time, except when I run around with Black Gold. So tonight I decided to have a good inspection of the rugs in the front room. My mum is mad about rugs, rugs and plants are everywhere in the house. Anyway I was telling you that we were left alone for a few hours, my sisters each went to a different room upstairs so I was left all alone downstairs, and took advantage of that to check the rugs out one by one.

One rug in particular attracted my attention. Perhaps rather too much.

I like playing with rugs, I like it very much. I play with the ends of a rug, I like to camouflage myself with the ends. I build tunnels. I mess about with one end, then I do just the same with the other end. And all of a sudden the middle of the rug lifts up and creates a tunnel in which I can hide and ambush anyone passing by. It's so much fun!!

Tonight one of the rugs gave me trouble. I looked at it, and looked at it again, and I decided that something needed to be done with it. It's square, a terracotta colour with some sort of

Greek design and it has (had) fringes on both sides. I started sorting the fringes on one side and then got very busy with the other side. I worked on it, and kept working on it. It was a very strange and rewarding job. It's simple, if I put one of my claws in one of the fringes and pull, it comes off. It does, I'm telling you, it does!

So I kept busy trying one fringe, then another, then another. Then I wanted to figure out how on earth a rug is made. So, once I got most of the fringes out of one side, I decided to investigate the warp and weft. And I pulled, and pulled, and pulled. I kept busy all evening, all the time my mum was away. I thought I was doing a good job because as the fibres were coming off, I was a really good boy and organised them all in a little heap on one side. Truly, I kept the whole thing very tidy, all in one little heap. I'm good at these things.

When my mum came back, it was rather late. Gosh, did she look tired. I wonder where she'd been? She'd been to disco. Hmmm, disco at her age? She's past the sell-by-date for any disco stuff, I'm sure. I walked towards mum to greet her in the corridor. She picked me up and gave me a big hug (I thought she wanted to suffocate me) and she said lots of beautiful things. I felt so great and I thought to myself, "Wait till she sees the good job I've done tonight."

Black Gold came downstairs and she also got a big hug and plenty of kisses. Gosh, that kid loves fuss, I tell you, man, she just loves fuss.

My mum then walked into the front room. I heard her saying, "What on earth is that?" Only the side lamp was on at the time. On went the main central light. Mum saw the little pile

of fringes and fibres and fluff that I'd made and I was right
behind her. She didn't need to call me that loud, I'm not deaf.
She shouted, "Sir Norman!"

"Hey you, I'm here, I'm just behind you."

She turned to me and started laughing, laughing a lot. What's
the point of putting so much effort into tidying up all my
work into a neat pile if I don't get compliments, only laughter,
can someone tell me? My mum picked me up in her arms and
asked me if I didn't like this particular style. She also told me
she'll stop some of my pocket money to pay to replace the
rug. Do you think she means that?

Lots of love from Sir Norman

25. Can anyone help?

Hello my Wild Berry friends,

Maybe you can help me. I'm getting increasingly concerned because I can't find my dad. Maybe you know where he is?

It's been a few days now since he went missing. At first I was just too busy to worry about it and I also thought he's gone visiting friends and he'll be back soon but he hasn't come back yet and I'm wondering where he is.

I did search a bit today but I've had no luck so far in finding him. Also, for the past couple of days I've been sleeping in front of his study door. I thought to myself that if he comes back in the middle of the night, I'll be the first to know if I sleep by his door! But he hasn't turned up.

Just after midnight I woke the whole house up. I was happy with that attention! At last! My sister Black Gold came to see what on earth I wanted and mum got up too. I was under my dad's desk shouting to see if he was hiding under his desk or behind some shelves in his study. I thought if I shouted loud enough he'd hear me and let me know where he was. No luck at all but I had a cuddle from mum so I was happy for a little while.

At one o'clock this morning I decided enough is enough and maybe my dad's under the blankets. I jumped on the bed where my sister Pirate was sleeping with mum, and you know what, she never even chased me off the bed! Truly, she just took a look at me and then kept watching what I was doing. I can't believe not being chased by Pirate. Anyhow, it was obvious that dad wasn't under the blankets, I looked but there was nothing there.

Then I saw that next to mum's head there were two pillows, one on top of the other, and I thought that's where he's hiding, I've got to look under those pillows and between them, I was sure that's where he must be. So I started to search by pulling and pulling the pillows. They're quite big so I couldn't manage to pull them onto the floor. Then I had another idea and, instead of pulling them, I just put my head under the first one. But no, nothing there. Then I put my head under the second one. Gosh, that's a bit more effort, I thought, this is so much weight to lift up on my neck and shoulders but somehow I managed. But, no, nothing there either.

I pushed and pushed mum so I could see under her pillow. No, nothing again. Mum was then sitting on the bed so I parked myself between her pillow and her back, which gave me time to think. After a little while I decided to suddenly jump from the bed to my dad's bedside table. Well, my legs work very well now! But I was so frustrated at not finding him that I had a bit of a temper tantrum. I threw everything on dad's table onto the floor, including the alarm clock; such a noise it made in the middle of the night. Then I jumped from my dad's side table straight onto the floor. Another noise like a bomb going off! My mum was trying to get hold of me. She had a bit of a hard time but in the end she managed it. She just wanted to give me another cuddle but I was so frustrated that I swore at her and I also bit her arm, so she had to let me go.

I miss my dad. There's no one to call me 'mate', no one other than him shortens my name to Norm, there are no John Wayne videos playing, nothing's going on in this house. So if my dad happens to turn up at Wild Berry can you let him know that I'm looking for him?

Best thoughts,
a very annoyed Sir Norman

26. I am good at pirouettes and opera

Hello Nico, Val and Melissa,

How are you doing? I'm pleased to tell you that I found my dad. Poor thing, when I jump on his lap, he rattles with all the pills he's taking. I won't go into any details right now though.

Just a quick note to tell you something funny.

I've taken to liking food like crazy! I often hear my mum telling dad that I eat like a little horse, I just love my food enormously. The food is really good here, I can have what I want. Mum goes to such lengths to keep everyone happy. I have my own food; one brand has a cat's name, the other brand has the same name as my moustache; ocean selection, super-meat, meat selection, a variety of biscuits.

My dad's always worried that I'm still growing so I need feeding up. Mum's always worried that if I get fed too much, I'm going to put on too much weight, which of course wouldn't be good for my legs. So when it comes to food and meal times, there's always a parliamentary discussion between mum and dad. As long as I get fed, it's OK by me if they have a political debate on the subject!

Anyway, besides the food matter, I wanted to let you know that I'm now so happy that I make everyone at home laugh at meal times, because this is the best time for me to show off my talent at opera and pirouettes. I don't know why, I can't explain it but I get so excited about the good food that I sing really loud (you remember the sounds that I can make with my voice, don't you?!). I start singing as soon as mum prepares the food in the kitchen. I've got my own plates and bowls, no one else uses them, they're all for me, so I know the sounds they make. I recognise them even if I'm far away and I rush back to the kitchen and wait for mum to prepare the food.

I'm very patient waiting for it to be ready but then when mum turns round and shows me my plate and my bowl, I can't help it, I get so excited, I sing loud and I keep on spinning round and round. Mum says I do the best pirouettes and dad calls me Pavarotti. I sing and dance all the way to the dining room. Yes, the dining room is where I have my meals. They tried to feed me in the kitchen with my sisters but I get too nervous about the Queen Bee, so I don't eat. Dad said that too much happened to me earlier in my life for food to be a worry or disrupted, and if I don't like eating in the kitchen I should have my own place in the dining room, so that's where I have my meals. I have my own mat, behind the plants, so it's very peaceful there, I can eat what, when and as much or as little as I want, it's my very own place.

So from the kitchen to the dining room I amuse everyone present with my personal show. Twice a day I keep my mum and dad amused!

All for now, speak soon.

Lots of love,
Sir Norman

27. In the kitchen

Good morning my friends at Wild Berry,

I had such a fright! I've got to tell you all about it.

I'm starting to learn about life now so it's not that I'm so impressed by new things. Or let's say I can now stand up for myself and defend myself quite well. But, boy, that was a scare.

Mum had a friend visiting the other day. Nothing wrong with that but the friend brought several things along and one was e-n-o-r-m-o-u-s. At first I thought nothing of it, I was too busy minding my own business in the garden to be worried about it then. They had a cup of tea, you know, as people do, and chat, chat, chat.

Then mum's friend left and I got a good dose of, "What a good boy" and this and that. As long as it keeps people happy, I'm happy. But, gee, sometimes human beings are funny, they talk to me in such a funny voice. They're unable to use their own normal, voice. No, no, they have to use a voice as if I were a baby, you know what I mean? "What a good boyyyyyyy." I tell you!

Anyway, the lady left, mum was busy in the kitchen, and I went back to what I was doing. I'm so very busy these days. I was on the patio and I could see that mum put some of the stuff that her friend brought in the fridge. I wonder what humans use those things for? Soon it'll be dinner time for us, I thought, but it was a nice day so I decided to stay outside a little longer. But I often stop what I'm doing to go and see mum or dad. They're always doing something different and I also like to remind them that I'm here. Besides, I always get a cuddle or my dad shakes paws with me and always asks me, "Where are you going, mate?" He's so funny, so I go back indoors quite often.

That day, as I told you earlier, I spent the afternoon outside and, seeing my mum moving about in the kitchen, I thought I'd go and see for myself what she was doing but, most important, I went to check the situation on the dinner plate front, and which cupboard doors were opening. I've worked out, depending on which door is opening, or if the dinner plates are being moved, whether or not it's a good sign that food is about to be served.

So here I was on my way to the kitchen door.

Gosh, what's that?

What the hell is on the floor?

Have you seen that?

I'd never seen such a huge thing.

I was petrified, I kept on staring at it. What if it moves? Can this thing move? If it does, I'm done man, I tell you that right now, I'm done! It's so big, no way am I going be able to stand up to it, no way!
This thing must be at least three times as big as me. Gee, I just hope it doesn't move as I go past.

All these thoughts were going on in my head and I realised

that I hadn't moved! I was still frozen by the kitchen door, couldn't put one leg in front of the other to cross the kitchen. I started to move my neck and shoulders, my back was lowering, and my legs were ready to spring, just in case this thing moved. It's so huge. I started to move my legs and, without knowing it, I took a step forward. What if this thing moves? I took another step. I'm so brave, considering the size of this thing. I heard my mum calling dad, "Come and have a look at this." Well, I was pleased about that as I knew for sure that with my dad there, if this thing were to make a move, he'd be strong enough to stop it flattening me.

I ventured out closer to it and with my front leg I tried to touch this thing. Now that dad was around, I felt safe. I stretched my arm a little more, ooohhhh, just a little more. My neck was stretching too, and my eyes were growing bigger than my head. I've never seen such a big thing on the kitchen floor. I thought it was a big snake, not that I've ever seen a snake, but I thought this is what they must look like. And I heard something on the TV about dinosaurs, so I thought this might have been a baby one, who knows?

Then mum picked me up and told me it was a marrow. They eat such things, humans do, I'm told.

It's still on the kitchen floor. Every time I pass by the place, I can't help being cautious, and I take quite a few steps sideways, just to avoid this thing as much as possible. You never know. The sooner mum takes it away, the better and safer I'll feel. It was a very scary experience.

Best thoughts to you all,
Sir Norman

28. The beauty parlour

Dear Nico,

A man-to-man conversation again. I'm having difficulties understanding all the time it takes to look after women.

You've known my sisters for a few years now, but do you have any idea how much time is spent looking after them? Do you have the remotest idea?

Well, not so much Pirate really. She gets looked after pretty well, mum combs her, sometimes dad does it too, but that's as far as it goes with Pirate. But the other one, Princess Precious, do you have any idea what goes on with her?

She gets washed every day, yeah, every day man! When she's not too well, she gets washed twice a day, morning and evening, the same circus twice a day. The water needs to be the right temperature, then she's put on one of dad's old T-shirts, then she gets washed, then dried.

If she's having a difficult time (you know when she has a crisis), dad turns up and helps, he keeps her occupied by talking to her while mum gets on with the washing. Man, you've never seen such a thing!

When she gets combed it's almost the same fuss. She whinges all the time, but she stays put, she knows that her fur needs to be combed to stay beautiful and shiny, so the brat whinges all the time but puts up with it all. Almost every time after she's combed, she goes and finds one of mum's jumpers or scarves or anything of mum's, and lies on it. She smells so much of perfume, I can't even start to describe how smelly she is. She just loves it, she does it every time.

My sister Black Gold also loves the smell of mum's make-up. I tell you, she's a real girl. When mum's not looking, dad gets hold of mum's make-up brushes and brushes Black Gold on her head and around her ears, on her whiskers. She could spend hours being pampered like that, she takes it all. Just try doing the same to Pirate, you'd see what happens. She wouldn't put up with it for anything, the old girl.

My dad says that Black Gold always smells very nice. For sure she does, she's precious and she knows it, so nice smells go well with the whole thing.

Now, no joke, but you should see her after she's been groomed and combed and looked after just like a fairytale princess would be. Talk about wiggling her bum, she parades. She lies with her front arms out as if she was posing for a photograph.

They spend hours looking after Black Gold. She's good fun though, my precious sister, we spend lots of time together now.

All the best for now,
Sir Norman

29. I'm only trying to help

Hello Wild Berry,

How are you doing? I found myself a little job. I just wanted to make myself useful around the house, there's so much to do. But I think I overdid it.

Seeing my mum always busy doing something in the house, I thought and thought, what can I do to make myself useful? Chasing spiders and flies, to start with, that seemed like a good idea.

I started with chasing spiders at night. With the patio doors open, they come in from the garden and run around the walls of the room. Their favourite hiding place is under the book-case. I know they always go for that place. They also try to hide under a pot plant or near it, but I'm very good at this little job and I always find them. I prefer the very big spiders. Mum hates them, but I'm so quick with my paws that they stand little chance with me.

I got so much praise for doing this job, from mum, and from dad, so much praise that I felt encouraged to do a bit more. So I decided to have a go at the flies. I'm good at this too but as their name suggests, they fly! Spiders walk and run or climb but they don't fly, so my experience accumulated with the spiders isn't always quite appropriate to chasing flies.

A couple of days ago, for instance, a fly was behind the sliding door net. I got a bit over-excited about this noisy little thing flying around and around. The more it flew, the more it got stuck between the door and the net. And it annoyed me too because my favourite place for sleeping is the armchair near the sliding door, and with this thing buzzing round and round, and round again, you couldn't sleep, I tell you. So anyway I said to this irritating fly, "I'm going to fix you", and hop, I took a big jump. The only thing was that the lacy net got in the way. This was a good thing really, because it helped me climb a bit higher, but there's a big hole in it now. Oooooops! I got the fly, though, so I got away with damaging the net.

This morning mum did all the hoovering, not that I like that noise very much but I put up with it. I stayed in dad's armchair while this noisy machine was going round the room. Gosh, I said to myself, my dad's got a lawnmower, my mum's got this hoover, I ask you, do human beings only have noisy toys? Mum hoovered the front room and all over downstairs, even the entrance hall (it's very light-coloured wood, so I can play football very well in the entrance hall). There's a very large plant in the entrance hall, it reaches the ceiling. It stands in a very large pot, a pot that even my two sisters and I couldn't make a circle round, the pot's so big that you'd have to tip it over to climb onto it.

When mum finished downstairs she started hoovering the stairs and when she reached the landing upstairs, she heard a noise. It was me trying to climb onto the dining table to chase a fly. So she gave me a cuddle and put me on an armchair, which meant (I knew immediately what it meant) I had to calm down and remain quiet for a little while. Fair enough, but how can I calm down and rest when there's another irritating fly buzzing around the room? So when my mum went back upstairs, I got off the armchair and did my job, the way I intended to. The point was, the more I tried to get this fly, the more agitated it became and it was flying like a mad thing, but I had no intention of giving up. First the fly tried to hide in a plant. The plant's not too high but it's got very large leaves which drop. Every time I tried to get the fly with my paw, I hit one of the leaves. I never meant to, but every time I did this, I shredded the leaf as if I was trying to make ribbons or fringes out of it. I tried several times and the more I tried the more the fly got mad, and the more cuts I made in the leaves.

I suspected I was doing something wrong, but what was the point of stopping, the objective was to get a result, the result was to neutralise the enemy, the enemy was the fly, and I was determined to get it.

All of a sudden, it flew out of the room! No way could I accept failure on a mission, that's not like me. So I looked round and round.

There it was!

It was in the mega large plant in the entrance hall. Hmmmm, that looks a bit high for me, I thought, I'm only tiny. Yeah, but I told you the pot's so big that you can easily stand on it, or better still, even get inside the pot. So I finished the job! I went back to my armchair, and now it was peaceful.

When my mum came downstairs, I heard her saying, "What on earth happened there?" Oh, oh, I said to myself, I think she's seen it. I could hear her talking to herself, asking what could possibly have happened. Oh, oh.

In my excess of goodwill in doing my utmost to get rid of that irritating useless fly, I'd climbed inside the huge pot. It's got a big pole right in the middle that the plant grows up, which is just as well, it's so big. The pole provided me with the best possible way to climb inside the plant and get the fly. The thing is, while climbing, I broke a few leaves. But the biggest problem was that, because I had to go around the pole several times, from the inside, things got a bit out of hand and I ended up depositing more soil on the floor than remained inside the pot. So out came the hoover again!

Just in case you're wondering, the fly was lying beside some broken leaves on the floor.

No, I wasn't pinned to the wall by mum. Yeah, I'm still alive.

When mum next saw dad, she asked him whether he liked the new designer plants in the house.
Now when mum sees a fly, she always opens the doors or windows and tries to chase the fly out with a cloth. I wonder why?

I'll let you know how I get on in my little job.

Lots of love,
Sir Norman

30. The international search

Dear Nico,

I know I only wrote to you yesterday, but I need help. I don't
understand women. It's not me, I tell you man, it wasn't me.
It's her again, it's all her fault. Yeah, her again, it's Black Gold.

What happened is, it's early morning, we were all out on the
patio, mum and dad were having a coffee, everything seemed
perfect. Pirate wasn't too far from me. Then Miss-Goody-
Two-Shoes-Princess-Black-Gold put in an appearance, wiggling her bum as usual. As her royal highness went by, I
looked at her. Well, I didn't just look at her, I must admit. She
went by me and looked at me as if I were very ordinary, so I
showed her my paw. I didn't have any boxing gloves on, but as
she was parading by me, I lifted my arm and showed her my
paw. I would've liked to belt her one. You know, not to hurt
her, just to scare her off, only to scare her off, I swear. I
didn't, I promise, I didn't touch her. I always tell the truth,
only the truth.

The point is, she did it again, yeah, she did it again. She created such a fuss, such a fuss, man. I can't believe women can
be so complicated. Are they all like that? Now, if I'd done that
to you, or you to me, we'd have lain in wait for the other one
round the corner, and then at some point in the day, wallop,
I'd have belted you a good one or you'd have belted me a
good one, right? That's how we'd have sorted it out as men,
right? Nothing more than that, nothing else, right? But,
women, they have to create a fuss. The more I get to know
them, the more I can see it happening every time, they create

a fuss, they just love it! The thing is that, today, she started an international search; Interpol, the CIA, MI5, 6, 7, 8 and I think 9 were also on the case. I tell you, man, it really felt like the entire universe was looking for Black Gold. Yeah, man, she decided to leave home. I'm telling you, man, that's what she did!

Mum called all of us for breakfast but only Pirate and I turned up, no Black Gold. They called and called her again and again but she wasn't having it, she wasn't going to show herself. Mum went down the garden and I tell you, man, you've never seen such a performance. Mum had Black Gold's plate with her breakfast in it in one hand and in the other hand she had a fork, and as she was walking down the garden she was calling Black and banging on the plate with the fork.

Then, even funnier, dad was going down the garden, behind mum, with a jar of biscuits in his hands, and the poor bloke was rattling the jar of biscuits. So one was banging the plate, the other was rattling the jar. What a pair, they looked like weird hunters. I wish I could've taken a photo, especially a photo of my dad, my dad rattling the jar of biscuits. If only the people he works with, or, better still, the people working for him, could've seen him; talk about losing credibility.

Anyway, with all this circus going on, the little precious gem never turned up, so back they went to the kitchen. Mum thought she'd come back pretty soon. But no, no, she didn't. Mum went back to the bottom of the garden and 'Eureka' she saw Black, yeah, she saw her. So what, you might add? Yeah, mum saw Black but the little darling was on the other side of the fence. At that point, I'd got to the middle of the garden and I was sitting there quietly. I thought to myself, I'm going to get such a telling off again, the sooner it happens, the sooner it's over with. But mum and dad were so worried about Princess Wiggly Bum they just forgot about me.

Black Gold had managed to get out but couldn't get back. She thinks she's so clever, but she can do one thing but can't do it in reverse. Good job she doesn't drive a car. She drives *me* mad but doesn't drive a car, she'd never be able to reverse it. Typical woman!

It was clear she was getting increasingly distressed, she was yelling and running about in any and every direction. My dad was concerned because she was running towards the railway. I bet your bottom dollar that dad was most concerned about himself, I'm sure he was also thinking that he was going to get a telling off because the princess went over the fence. He also thought, the quicker I get that little devil back, the sooner I get told off and the quicker it's over with. I bet that's what dad was thinking.

Anyway, remember I told you that the very first couple of days I lived here, I went into next door's garden? Remember? Well, since that day, dad fixed the fence so well that it is i-m-p-o-s-s-b-l-e, I repeat *impossible*, to climb over it now. So how on earth she got over the other side, no one will ever know (I do, I showed her my paw!). So dad had to climb the fence and go into next door's garden, then from their garden, over their fence into the fields. Naturally, by then the little darling had disappeared! I'm exhausted just retelling the events.

Mum was so worried about Black, she couldn't take it any longer, she went back into the kitchen. Dad was in next door's garden, the poor bloke was hoping that the little darling would make it back to their garden and that he wouldn't have to walk down to the railway where people could see him. No such luck.

To reassure mum, dad shouted to her from next door's garden that, no worries, he'd walk down to the railway and look in the fields and he promised he'd find Black Gold.

Mum was ever so worried. I saw in the newspapers that where we live quite a few four-legged creatures had disappeared and mum was beside herself.

Mum looked through the kitchen window. It was just a lost look into the distance, she wasn't even looking for anything in particular, she was just standing there, waiting. But she caught a glimpse of something black and white at the bottom of the garden. Did you say something black and white?! What did you say? Black and white?

Yep, the little darling was back. At the bottom of the garden. Standing there like a little angel. Mum went down the garden like a rocket. She picked up Black Gold and gave her loads of cuddles. I would've given her a good dose, not cuddles but, no, mum gave her lots of cuddles. Although I wanted to give her a good hiding, I went into hiding myself indoors. Mum was still at the bottom of the garden, now she was calling for my dad. What a circus. First they go down in a ceremonial procession calling for Black Gold, then she's calling for my dad. Mad house, complete mad house.

My dad couldn't hear a thing so mum went back into the kitchen and fed Black Gold. All this time and dad still wasn't back. Black Gold went upstairs after breakfast to sleep on mum's table and dad still wasn't back. Then, after quite a while, he turned up. He looked like a lost soul. He had to admit to mum that he hadn't managed to find Black Gold. The poor bloke said that he went all the way down to the railway, up to the bridge. That means that he walked from our house up to the middle of the village, crossing several gardens in the process and he said that some people looked at him crossing their gardens.

I was sure that it'd now be mum's turn to feel a bit, you know, just a bit awkward because how on earth was she going to tell dad that Black Gold had turned up, had her breakfast and was already asleep, while all this time dad was still looking for her? When mum told dad all about it, I was sure the bloke would want to kill someone or break something, just to calm his nerves, so I watched him from a distance.

I just can't believe that all this fuss happened just because I showed Black Gold my paw. Did she need to create such a pandemonium?

No, Nico, in case you're wondering if either I or my dad got a ticking off, no, we didn't. Mum was far too happy at having everybody back safely. We were confined to the house, though, for the rest of the day.

I really can't understand women. I know I should leave Black Gold alone but I can't help it. But you tell me, does she need to be like that? I'll see you around Nico,

Sir Norman

31. I'm gonna have that bird

Dear all at Wild Berry,

Just an update on my activities. I'm doing pretty well on my back legs and this allows me to add daily activities to my schedule that's getting busier and busier by the day.

Hunting. I'm seriously considering getting a good education in this particular activity. I'm now allowed to spend more and more time in the garden. But I've learned that when I get a little over-zealous and go too far down the garden, mum comes out of the kitchen and reminds me NOT to go too far. She does that every time, so now I still go down the garden but when I see mum coming, I walk back.

There are so many birds in this garden, man, I've never seen so many! The point is that both mum and the lady who lives next door are mad about animals, so even the birds get spoiled! They don't cut the ivy growing over the fence, so the birds can nest in it, they don't cut the brambles, so the birds can feed on the berries. There are thousands of birds here, thousands!

There might be thousands but I'm only interested in half a dozen. Really round, chubby, fat birds, there are only just a few of these – doves! They look like chickens, they're so big. Just like chickens, and so appetising. Now, don't go thinking that I'm not fed here, that's not true. I get fed whatever and whenever I want. It's just the buzz, the buzz of getting to hunt. I hide behind a tree or a plant and then I jump out of nowhere. I haven't succeeded yet, but I will, I will soon. I'm not interested in small sparrows or similar creatures, what's the point? It's a lot of effort hunting and for what? Such a small bird? Not worth it! I'm going to have a dove. Mum already caught me several times rather too close to one, and every time she calls me, she spoils the game, she really does!

In the past few days, I even tried climbing up a tree to be closer to my prey but I can't quite make it up the tree. I'll have to wait a bit longer to be able to do that, but even so I know I'll have one of those birds very soon.
I'll let you know when it happens!

Lots of love to you all,
Sir Norman

32. In the bathtub

Dear all at Wild Berry,

I've got to write to you to tell you something, you'll never guess what happened today, you'll never be able to guess!

Black Gold (yeah, her again) has had to have a bath. Just like mum does. Truly, they put her in the bathtub. I'm going to tell you all about it.

This morning dad looked through the window, and he calls mum, "Come and have a look, quick, something's wrong with Black Gold. Something's really wrong, she looks like a drowned rat." Call Black Gold a rat? The man's mad. Call the princess a rat and that means real big trouble with mum. Mum takes a look and, yes, it was true the little darling was wet, but there was no way she looked like a rat. Mum thought nothing much of it, it was early morning, there was quite a lot of morning dew on the grass and she thought it was as simple as that, simple as that.

We were called for our breakfast. Then, "What the heck is that smell?" Mum was going around trying to find out where this horrible smell was coming from. She called dad and then both of them were trying to track down the smell. In the meantime we ate our breakfast.

Black Gold happened to pass by mum. Mum was a bit concerned now that she was still rather wet. It wasn't a particularly warm day outside. Dad told mum she should see to her. (See to her?) Mum picked up the little darling, then said,

"What the heck? Where? What have you done?" Dad came back into the kitchen. It was obvious by then that, yeah, you guessed it now, that horrible smell was Black Gold. Talk about being posh, talk about parading! Dad said to mum, "Not only does she look like a drowned rat, she's also wearing Sewage Flower No. 5." I tell you, she was in a state. Her fur was all greasy and clogged up but the worst of it was the smell, the smell, it was terrible.

It was a very distinctive smell but neither mum nor dad could figure out what it was. Dad thought that someone threw dirty water over Black. Mum said that wasn't possible because our garden is not really accessible from the outside. Dad went all over the garden trying to pick up clues but in vain.

Before I proceed, I have to tell you that Black Gold is prone to 'miss'-haps. If something happens, it has to happen to Black Gold, no one else but Black Gold. My dad told me that once upon a time they used to live in a different house where the kitchen was huge and mum decided to have designer chairs. ("Your mother's idea, mate, not mine," my dad told me.) These chairs had curved legs and almost every time Black jumped on the chair, nine times out of ten, the chair would overturn. One day mum heard a bang louder than usual. She went into the kitchen and once more the chair was over-turned.

Then Black Gold couldn't eat biscuits for a couple of days. Mum thought she'd gone off them but on the third day, knowing how greedy Black is, mum decided to inspect Black Gold's mouth and found the little darling had the imprints of her teeth in her lips and her lips were four times as big as usual because they were swollen. So she must have banged herself so hard in missing the chair that to this day dad talks about that episode and to this day he can't explain how on earth she never broke her canines. Naturally, the chairs had to go!

Anyway, returning to the smell, mum and dad looked all over the place but couldn't find out what that specific smell was.

Black Gold was placed in the kitchen sink, my dad held her back legs and mum washed her with a tissue and they thought it was all done. Black Gold was sent upstairs to mum's room and both mum and dad thought that in drying out, the smell would go away.

But my dad kept investigating. The patio was entirely dry, except for a wet patch under the overflow. Dad called mum, the smell was coming from there. It turned out that mum put the central heating on just that day, but she forgot to bleed the radiators, the system was full of pressure and the fluid got out of the system through the overflow. Black Gold, prone to *ca-tastrophe*, happened to be under the overflow and that was the smell. So explanation found, that was the end of the matter, right? End of the matter? You've got to be kidding.

Both mum and dad went upstairs to see Black Gold; the stench in mum's room was unbearable. I went upstairs behind dad, so I was there too and the smell was terrible. In drying out the smell had got even more pungent than when she was wet. Mum felt her stomach turning, the smell was that bad.

The decision was taken there and then, Black Gold would have to have a bath. The water was run in the bathtub, bubble bath added and Goody-Two-Shoes was put in the water. I was still there, witnessing all of it. I was also worried, asking myself, "Are we going to get this as well?" I was thinking of Pirate and myself, "Are we going to have a bath too?" I'll run behind the sofa. But, no, I stayed there to watch everything going on with Black Gold. She was completely wet by then. I could hear the water splashing and splashing while mum was washing her. She wasn't too happy but it could've been worse, she tried once or twice to escape from the water but mum reassured her, so she stayed.

I felt sorry for her. Have you ever seen a completely wet cat? Talk about looking like a rat. She no longer looked like a cat, her front legs became so skinny, it was painful to see. She had front legs the size of a bread stick. Her neck was as tiny as one of my dad's fingers. Have you ever seen a wet cat? Such a state, man!

Eventually she came out of her smelly water. "What do you look like?" I asked her. I tell you, she wouldn't look at me, she wouldn't look at me at all, she was looking the other way, she was so embarrassed. Mum put a huge bath towel around her, then she looked like a giant sausage! How very funny the whole thing was.

Black wasn't happy looking like a giant sausage, she managed to get set free on the floor and guess what she did next. She escaped from the bathroom and went straight to lie down in her litter tray, true man, she lay down in her litter. She was still pretty wet, not dripping any more but wet, so she had bits of litter stuck up all over her legs, her belly, you name it, she had litter all over the place. I couldn't help looking at her, completely stunned. "What do you look like?" I asked her, "Look at you!" Mum was fighting with the litter as she was trying to

111

dry her with the towel but dad told her she'd better get the hairdryer out, which she did. Black wasn't too happy at first but then she was OK. Talk about a beauty parlour. The entire morning was spent around that little brat. And then talk about smelling nice afterwards.

Also talk about parading afterwards. One of mum's friends turned up after it was all over, and she couldn't believe how silky and nice Black's fur was. Mum explained everything that had happened and the lady was saying, "How very beautiful you are, what a pretty girl." I was trying to get some of this attention; Black Gold doesn't need so many compliments, she knows she's pretty, she certainly doesn't need to be reminded of it. I wanted to tell the lady that she should've seen Black a few hours earlier and should've smelt her too, but no one was paying any attention to me. Women fuss again!

Lots of love,
Sir Norman

33. Rescuing the bird in the kitchen walls

Dear all at Wild Berry,

I've got to tell you what happened here the other day. You're never gonna believe it, but it happened! And you'd better sit down and have a cup of tea as this is going to be quite a story.

As I told you in one of my previous letters, there are lots and lots of birds here, truly, loads of them. The majority are little birds like sparrows or robins. The smaller they are, the less brain they have, I believe, especially the youngest ones; they've got no experience, they know nothing of life, so they get themselves into so much trouble.

On the roof of the house there's a chimney, on the side wall of the house, on the kitchen side, it looks like a big box with steam coming out of it. When it's windy or raining, the birds look for a place to hide, soooooo, yeah, you guessed it, they use the chimney. The thing is that the house has double walls with a cavity in between. In most cases, the birds get away all right but on this occasion there was pandemonium.

Mum started hearing a bird in the kitchen boiler so she calls dad. Dad couldn't hear it. Mum hears it again. Dad still can't.

Mum calls her friend to come round. She does. They're all in the kitchen – mum, dad, the friend, Black Gold and my little self. Complete silence. Nothing happens. No one speaks. I look at Black Gold, "What are they all doing?" I asked, "Is this some sort of game for grown-ups?" Everybody kept quiet. Then there it was, the bird in the boiler again. That was it!

They all heard it this time, mum wasn't gaga after all.

The friend leaves. Dad takes the boiler apart … nothing.

They waited and waited and waited but nothing, no more noise, nothing at all. The boiler was put back together again. Everyone went back to their own business. Everyone except mum. She knew the bird was still there, she just knew it.

After a little while the noise started up in the boiler again. That was it, no more excuses, mum called British Gas, the emergency team. Dad told her, "You're going to be popular. Who's going to tell the engineer there's a bird in the boiler?" But mum wasn't going to have another word said about it, she couldn't leave the bird to roast in the boiler.

The engineer turned up. As it was an emergency, he'd driven all the way from Hastings on the coast. Mum was busy on the phone when the engineer rang the bell so Dad had to answer the door. "My wife thinks there's a bird in the kitchen boiler," I heard dad saying, he was so embarrassed he was speaking through his teeth.

The gas man was so big, a huge man, you should have seen the look on his face. "A bird in the boiler?" He reluctantly made his way to the kitchen. He had a big case full of tools and he spread them all out on the kitchen floor. And then started to take the boiler apart, again.

There was no way that the bird, poor soul, was going to reveal himself while the gas man was around, no way. The man was so very noisy, he was annoyed as well and I think that added to the level of noise he was making. So, the bird never showed up and the gas man left. Dad asked mum, "I wonder what this guy is going to put on his work report sheet? Attended a house with a bird in the boiler?" I think dad was getting annoyed too. I'm not sure he completely believed mum, even though her friend had been in the kitchen when there was that noise. Dad said to mum that maybe it was just a vibration from the boiler. NO WAY, mum said, there was a bird in there and she knew it!

An hour or so went by. Then, there it was, that noise again!

At that point mum was determined not to say anything more to dad. She realised that there's a vent on the kitchen wall and the vent has a little sliding door. Mum opened the door and she could see the bird through the vent. Mum discreetly went to the garage to get some of dad's tools and came back with a screwdriver the size of a cannon. She started to unscrew the vent on the wall, yeah, truly. As she started her building works, Black and I looked at each other thinking, gee, that means trouble, trouble big time. Black was looking worried, "Oh, oh," she said "good job dad knows nothing about all this."

The vent came off the wall and now there was a big hole in the wall. I didn't want to even start thinking about dad's comments if he were to see what was going on behind his back. The bird was going backwards and forwards in the hole. It was now very clear that there was a cavity in between the walls and every time mum tried to go nearer the hole, the bird retreated into the cavity. When she walked away from the hole, the bird would reappear but would never venture out.

That was real entertainment, I can tell you, man! To try and gain the bird's trust, mum put some pieces of bread in the hole so that the bird could smell it, come nearer the opening, see more of the daylight, and fly away. That was plan A. Do human plans always go according to schedule? The lights were off, the window and the kitchen door were wide open, the bread was in position, we were completely silent. Plan A was about to succeed.

"What on earth are you lot doing?"

The three of us, mum, Black and me, we jumped three feet high. No one heard dad coming in, he scared the hell out of us. No one spoke. Black Gold made a move towards the corridor. All mum could say was, "Well, the bird won't come out now, will it?" That was for sure, the bird withdrew even deeper in between the two walls.

There was silence for a while, then mum made a cup of tea. Both mum and dad decided not to put the vent back on the wall for the time being.

Dad went out onto the patio, where he found Black Gold all agitated. She was frantic, she was pacing up and down where the pipes from the sink came out of the wall. Dad called mum, of course, "What on earth is she going on about now?" he said. Both mum and dad stood there, looking at Black Gold, not saying anything.

She was really frantic, trying to get up the pipe, stretching her body to the top of the pipe, what a performance. Mum went closer, Black was trying to say something to mum. The more mum asked Black what the matter was, the more my sister would shout and yell. Mum went up really close to the pipes. Have you guessed?

She could hear the bird clearly now! I was witnessing all this kerfuffle. Actually I was enjoying myself, never a dull moment in this house! At this point dad could no longer say he couldn't hear the bird.

Off the pipes came from the wall. Dad went back into the kitchen and off came the pipes and the water system from under the sink.

Now there were several holes in the kitchen, the one on the wall and one under the sink, and now also on the outside kitchen wall, there was a hole where the pipes had been. More bread was put into the outside hole. Mum and dad stood there in complete silence, waiting for that poor bird to come out of his walled prison.

Ah, there he is. He was a tiny creature, frightened to death, he was on the edge of the outside hole, shouting his head off, he was too scared to come out of it.

This is one of those stories that make me very tired just retelling it. And it ain't finished yet!

Dad went back indoors to read his newspaper and he told us, "When it's all over call me." Mum was talking to sis and me when all of a sudden this little bird flew out of the hole.

You'll never guess what he did next. You'll never guess, some mothers do have 'em! When he tried to leave the outdoor hole, he flew off but far too low for Black Gold to miss such a golden opportunity and she jumped up and tried to catch him. The kitchen door was still open and he was so scared that instead of flying high, he did a U-turn and flew straight back into the kitchen. I said to myself, "This one will never learn, will he? He's thick as a plank."

He flew back into the kitchen and this time found refuge behind the fridge. I know, I know, it's hard to believe, right? If someone told me all this, I'd find it hard to believe too, but it's true, I was there. He fluttered about behind the fridge and then decided to park himself at the foot of it, you know, where the motor is. On each side of the motor there's an empty space for the air to circulate, right, and he decided to park there, by which time he was exhausted. Black Gold could see him from the outside, through the aerating holes. She was flat out on the floor and this poor bird was terrified on the other side of the mesh.

By then dad had made a reappearance in the kitchen. He was looking on one side of the fridge, Black Gold was shouting on the other, as if she was telling him, "Dad, you're looking at the wrong side." What a show.
Can you use your imagination and visualise what the kitchen looked like by then? Let me remind you; the vent was off the wall leaving a huge gaping hole, all the bits and pieces from under the sink were on the kitchen floor to allow dad to undo the pipes under the sink, the outside pipes (one of which had got broken in the process) were scattered on the patio, and the fridge was now being pulled away from the wall, into the middle of the kitchen. It looked like a building site!

Black Gold kept on shouting to dad that he was looking at the wrong side. I kept myself parked to one side, this was such good entertainment that I didn't want to miss any of it. Eventually, dad got the bird and went to the bottom of the garden and put him on the garden shed so that he could recover in peace. He did fly away a few minutes later, safely. Do you think this is the end of the saga? Dad started putting every-thing back into place. The vent went back on the wall but the tiny screw covers were left off, just in case there was another bird caught up in there. The pipes under the sink were put back but because one of the joints was a little old, it was leak-ing. The outside pipe was replaced but it got broken in the process. It was evening by then and dad was a little sarcastic for the rest of the day.

In the morning dad went to the plumbing suppliers to buy the pipes and joint to replace the old ones. When he came back, he had the plumber's bill in his hands and he called Black Gold. "Next time Black, do me a favour," said dad to my sis, "do me a favour and eat the bird straight away."

I tell you, in this house, there's never a dull moment. Good job not all moments are as extreme as this 'save the bird' episode.

Lots of love,
Sir Norman

34. Gone fishing

Good morning,

I'm writing a little note to you because, once again, I was told off. Next door, there's a pond in the garden, hidden by lots of plants and flowers around it, so no one can see me.

I got into the habit of going next door to inspect the pond. There are so many fish in there; plop, plop, plop, I can hear the fish coming to the surface to eat or play, it's such a temptation. Every day this week I went there and every day I was in trouble, but I can't help it, the temptation's so strong.

Dad laughs at me and says to mum that one day she'll see me coming up from the bottom of the garden with a fish in my teeth. Mum told me it'd be much cheaper if I let her go to the supermarket and get me some fish, so that I'd leave the expensive one next door alone, but I just can't help it!

That shows that my legs are getting stronger and stronger, I can now climb over the fence. Dad said today, "Another job to do." He needs to go and put up some higher panelling, I guess. But I'd get over that too! I'd love to get one of those fish. Will keep you informed.

Lots of love,
Sir Norman

35. The barbie

Dear all at Wild Berry,

I want to tell you all about the barbie. It's her again, it's Black Gold, not that she looks like Barbie, but she created a fuss again today.

Now, just because I said the barbie, don't you go thinking things, OK? I know my credit cards were cut off some time ago but that doesn't necessarily mean that I'm now playing with dolls. I can see you from here thinking things, yeah, truly, I can see you with your suspicious minds.

When I say barbie this, in Aussie language, means the barbe-cue! My dad has a barbie in the garden, one of those big barbies, a real one. It's a drum cut lengthways that stands on some iron beams, you know what I mean? Well-bred people would say it's a bushman cooker. Well, it is really! The drum's open on one side and that's where dad puts the wood. You'll understand later why I told you this particular detail.

Anyway, it all started because mum was doing her plants. She cut a few overgrown leaves here and there and, as I was lying outside on the patio, she gave me a long branch that she'd cut off one plant. I always play with anything and everything so mum gave me the branch to play with.

Out of nowhere came Goody-Two-Shoes-Princess-Beautiful and, of course, she wanted the branch too. Now, I'd say she's far too posh to play with any toy at all, let alone a branch. But, no, just to be a pain in the you-know-what, she wanted the branch that I'd been given. So she started grabbing the branch from one end, while I had hold of it by the other end. It was my branch in the first place, so why should she have it? The branch wasn't very long, about a foot, a foot and a half at the most, and I sat on one end of it while my sis tried to get hold of it from the other end. Then she decided to sit on it as well, at her end, which meant that we were sitting rather close together. This could've gone on for ever as she wanted the branch and I wasn't going to let go.

I've learnt to stand up for myself so, what did I do? I just showed her my paw, simple as that, but it works. I tell you man, it works. I just sit there, raise my right arm just a little above my head, open my paw wide so that it looks bigger than it really is, and show it to my sister. She spits at me and she whinges. All I do is show her my paw, but she's impressed, very impressed, so she leaves with a huff and a puff, and as usual she screams.

The point is that she did it again, she created a fuss. She jumped into the barbie, yep, she jolly well did! Mum saw everything except where Goody-Two-Shoes went. I knew where she was, but said nothing.

For a little while mum looked here and there for Black Gold but couldn't find her. She knew Black couldn't have gone that far, so she wasn't too worried. Mum told me not to fret about my sis. "She'll soon be back," she told me.

Mum was back in the kitchen when she saw me. She saw me trying to jump into the barbecue! I was trying real hard to stand on my legs and get inside but it wasn't as easy as it looked. My sister has very strong and, funnily enough, very long back legs. My dad often tells her she looks like a kangaroo – that's a change from Marilyn! So, with such strong legs, she can jump really high but it wasn't so easy for me because there was nowhere I could get a firm grip on with my arms. I tried a few more times but had to give up. Just as well!

Black Gold came out of the barbecue. You have to remember that the three of us, Black, Pi and I, are black on our backs and in a few other places, but our bellies and parts of our legs are completely white. Out of the barbie came Miss Sooty. She'd lain in the burnt wood and ashes so her belly was all black and grey and her little white socks and gloves were no longer white. I asked her, "Blimey, what do you look like, sister?" She wasn't too chuffed, I can tell you, she just wasn't. Talk about wanting to show off, she was in such a state. Serves her right really, don't you think?

You know what? This little episode happened early this afternoon, and right now Black Gold is sleeping on mum's desk with all her feet and hands up in the air. And even now, after all day running about in the garden, she's still grey from the soot. Serves her right!

I thought I'd make you laugh, knowing how precious she is, you should've seen her!

More soon, hardly a day goes by without something happening!

Lots of love,
Sir Norman

36. My motorbike

Dear Nico,

Since you operated on me to remove the steel scaffolding supporting my hips, I've been feeling well. I'm less aggressive as the steel pin no longer irritates me. I jump and run quite fast in the garden and I have running competitions with Black Gold under the supervision of the Queen Bee, whos gets tired just watching us run like maniacs.

I've developed a little habit, though. Every time I sit down for more than a few seconds, I need to stretch my right back leg. As you know, this was always the most damaged leg, so this is the one that I need to stretch. The thing is though, you see, I can't stretch it in the normal way. No, no, it's much better if I shake it hard. I need to make like I'm trying to start a motorbike!

Are you with me? Do you understand what I mean? You get on the bike, and then with your right foot you get onto the pedal to start the engine. That's what works best for my back leg. I do this quite a lot and my dad always laughs at it. So the other day, dad told me I could choose between a Ducati or a Moto Guzzi. Do you think there's an Italian influence in the house?

I'll let you know soon what I'm going to buy.

See you around soon,
Sir Norman

37. I like reading newspapers

Dear all at Wild Berry,

I've discovered a new passion in life. It's reading! Truly, I'm not kidding, I like newspapers a lot. My dad asked me if I wanted him to buy me the newspaper with page three but I told him that I read all the pages so he needn't bother to change his usual newspaper.

I read page after page but the point is that I need the entire room to do this. One page, then the second, then the third. I have a good look at the front, then I toss the page in the air with my legs, then I jump on it and do it all over again. Page after page after page.

What I also like very much is hiding under a page. Despite eating like a horse, I'm still tiny, so I can easily hide under a large page of the newspaper. Then I walk all over the room with this page on my back, it doesn't move, I just carry it around. My dad asked me how I do it. I don't know how I do it, it just happens, maybe I'm gifted. So I go around the room hiding under the page and I think no one can see me. It's a lot of fun, truly, I enjoy myself a lot.

Sometimes my dad has a shock when he comes downstairs in the morning, there are newspapers all over the place. Other times I can be quite tidy really. I was seen playing with a few pages one evening, and mum and dad left me playing with them when they went to bed so they knew there were news-paper pages all over the place. The morning after, mum came down first, and she saw me but she couldn't find any newspapers at all. Dad came down later and he couldn't find any newspapers either. They looked around the room. But I'd crinkled up all the newspapers and hid the pages I was playing with behind a plant pot. Dad couldn't believe it, nor could mum. Well, I just wanted to be tidy, that's all.

Lots of love from Sir Norman

38. I did a Houdini disappearing act

Dear all at Wild Berry,

It was so funny ... I disappeared for just a while.

No, no, it's not what you think. I promise, it's not what you're thinking. I didn't even leave the house, truly. I'll tell you all about it.

I don't know whether or not you're fed up with seeing that guy on the telly, you know the one I'm talking about? They talk about him every day on the news. Oh, come on, think harder, it's that guy who's suspended in the air in London, he's in a glass box, you know the one now? Everyone says he's very good at doing disappearing acts, so I thought I'd have a go at it too just to see if I could. And it worked, it truly worked. They looked for me everywhere but I couldn't be seen.

Before I tell you how I did it, I have to tell you something but it's a house secret so, please, promise it's just between you and me, right?

Mum has a collection of fluffy toys. They're everywhere; in the bedroom, in her work room, on the bookshelves and most of all on the back of the armchairs and the sofa. Now, you'll never guess how mum came to have so many fluffy toys. Yes, some of them she got from a friend or two, they know that she likes fluffy toys, but that's not the secret though. The secret is that mum gets her fluffy toys from dad. Yeah, yeah, but guess why. When he's in trouble, if he did something wrong and he's in real serious trouble, he might try to get away with it with some flowers but mostly with fluffy toys. The bigger they are, the bigger the trouble he was in! There is one particular teddy bear that sits at the dinner table, he's huge. He sits at the head of the table and he's called Mr. Arthur. Well, you tell me, how much trouble must my dad have been in that day? To bring home such a huge teddy? Say no more!

So there are all those fluffy toys on the back of the sofa; a large Persian cat, a koala bear, a tiger with her cub in her mouth. What else? Oh yes, another cat lying on his own pillow. I'm sure I'm forgetting some, there are so many!

Well, now, guess where I was? Yes! I was! I was in between those fluffy toys. I stayed there for quite a while and it was so amusing to see everyone looking for me, coming and going. And me being as good as gold, very amusing indeed!

See, that guy in his glass cage in the middle of London, all that fuss about him and what he does. You don't need to be making all that fuss, you just have to hide in between mum's fluffy toys and the job's done!

All the best for now, lots of love,
Sir Norman

39. Someone is doing it deliberately

Dear all at Wild Berry,

A couple of things happened in the past few days. I was really annoyed so I want to tell you all about it.

I've undertaken a number of small tasks and duties around the house and garden and I like doing things properly, just because when I do I get so much praise from mum and dad. As I said before, dad often tells me I'm like John Wayne on patrol.

The other day I was in the garden and I was doing my best to keep the leaves under control. Or so I thought. There's a very tall silver birch in our garden, with thousands and thousands of leaves. One leaf dropped, then another one, and another one and I was rushing from one leaf to the next. My mission was to keep the place as tidy as I could.

As I was rushing to one side, I could see another leaf dropping not far from where I was. Then, as I moved towards the other location, I could see a couple more leaves dropping behind me. And as I turned round, even more leaves dropped somewhere else. I was annoyed. I was majorly annoyed, man.

I looked up at the tree. I couldn't comprehend why so many leaves were dropping at the same time. As I was under the tree, more leaves dropped. Mum and dad watched the whole scene, they were laughing. That made me even more annoyed; how can they laugh when I had so much work to do? I was so frustrated that I was by now careering from one side to the other; this was creating so much additional work. I'm accustomed to making little piles. When I chew mum's rug in the front room, I'm very tidy at putting all the pulled fibres into a pile. And when I read newspapers I also put all the pages into a neat little pile, usually behind the plant pot. So it just came naturally to me to try to make a pile of leaves, but by now they were dropping all over the place. You know what? I was convinced there was someone in the tree dropping leaves on me deliberately, for sure there was.

I stormed inside the house and rushed upstairs to see my sister Black Gold. We spend so much time together now that when I don't know something I ask my sis Black. So I rushed upstairs to mum's room. As usual, Black was on mum's table. I jumped on the chair that's nearby and stretched my neck to see my sis. I won't even try to jump on the table as Black will spit and swear at me if I do, so I said to myself, "I need her to explain to me about the leaves, so don't upset her by trying to jump on the table."

So I was on the chair, and Black was sound asleep with one of her arms covering her face. She's really cute my sis, pretentious but cute. I shouted, "Oi, sister!" No reply. I shouted again, "Black Gold, listen to me." No reply. I said to myself, "I'll fix her now." I made a move to jump onto her table. I put my two front paws on it, and gee, before I knew it she was spitting at me. It worked anyway! When I feel ignored, I just have to do something that she doesn't like and immediately she reacts. It didn't fail this time neither. I said to Black that there must have been someone up in the tree branches amusing himself by dropping leaves on me. She looked at me in a suspicious way and I jumped down from the chair. I wanted to go back outside with Black, so she could see for herself what I was talking about. Black Gold followed me outside, and the wind was blowing in all directions scattering the leaves everywhere. I was so annoyed to see so much mess all over the place. I rushed again from one leaf to another, and Black looked at me as if I were nuts.

Dad picked me up and started to sing *The Autumn Leaves*. Well, it was my very first experience with autumn, I didn't know, did I?

Lots of love from Sir Norman

40. There's an intruder in the house

Good morning all,

Gosh, I had a false alarm! The other night I was watching TV with mum and dad. Dad was on the sofa, mum in her armchair and I was in my own armchair and both my sisters were upstairs. I can't remember what kind of programme it was we were watching but we were all sitting down together. As I wasn't interested in the programme, I fell asleep, sound asleep.

All of a sudden, I heard something. I thought I was dreaming. I turned over. A little while later, I heard those voices again. I couldn't be dreaming, could I?

As I was sitting there in my armchair, mum and dad were looking at me, and I was trying to come out of my deep sleep. There were those voices again, now I was certain that there was an intruder, I knew it, there was someone in the house. I sat up. I stretched my neck. I wanted to be able to hear better. Again, those voices.

Gosh, I thought, where are my sisters? I got up out of the armchair. I looked under the coffee table – nothing. I went to the front door. I was cautious, in case there was someone bigger than me, you have to be careful, you know. Nothing. As I was patrolling around, I kept hearing those voices again and again.

Who could it be?!

I roamed around all downstairs but couldn't find anything or anyone. But I knew I wasn't wrong, there was someone in the house, but where? I went back to my armchair. I made sure I wasn't making any noise so that I could hear clearly. Once I was settled, I didn't want to go back to sleep, in case the intruder came back to the house. While all these thoughts were going round in my mind, I posted myself on the edge of the armchair so that I could jump down quickly, in case I was needed.

Black Gold came down to see what it was all about. She was sitting in the middle of the room when, all of a sudden, there were the voices again. She turned to me, she was so casual, she didn't panic at all. I asked her, "Did you hear, did you hear sis?" She turned her head away.

"Ppffffffffff," she said.

"What do you mean 'ppfffffff'? There's an intruder in the house and all you can say is 'ppffffff'. What kind of attitude is that?" I asked her.

By then Dad was really laughing. Mum stroked Black and came to my armchair for a cuddle.

There was a thriller on the TV. It was dark, it was night, it was completely silent in a dark street. Gosh, I'm shivering just thinking about it. There was a cat miaowing. Rushing through an empty house where there had been a murder. So scary. I hope I don't have any nightmares about it later.

I'm still very scared about those voices.
I'll see you soon,
Sir Norman

41. Sunday lunch

Dearest all at Wild Berry,

Sunday lunches in my house are an institution. There has to be a really serious reason for mum not to cook Sunday lunch. And when my dad's away for work, the thing he misses most is his Sunday roast with his Yorkshire pudding. No kidding, he tells everyone that, truly, he does.

Anyway, every Sunday my sisters Pirate and Black Gold are aware that the roast is cooking in the oven and every Sunday they'll have lunch with mum and dad. Mum prepares a couple of additional little plates, and while mum and dad have their lunch at the table, my sisters have their lunch near the table, from their own little plates on the floor. I'm now included, of course, but there are so many things I'm still learning about here, that I'm not quite familiar with this ritual and I still prefer having my meals behind the plants in the front room. Today mum cooked roast beef. Gee, it smelt real good.

Black Gold is the funniest of my sisters. On Sundays dad calls her Miss Bisto. Because she sleeps upstairs, dad says that either she has a good clock in her belly and knows exactly when lunch is going to be served, or she smells the gravy being made. Without fail, every Sunday, she turns up in the kitchen when the roast is about to come out of the oven. Truly, this is why dad calls her Miss Bisto!

Today, mum dished out my sister's plates and as usual Black was there at the rallying point, ready for her Sunday lunch! She was really enjoying herself eating her roast beef with great gusto. Pirate was there too but she was at the other end of the kitchen, so the first one I saw was Black and her little plate full of roast beef. I decided to take a closer look and I went up close to my sister. She wasn't too happy about it but because she was so busy stuffing herself with the beef, she left me in peace! I forgot to tell you that mum prepared my own little portion of beef as well, but I was far too interested in being with Black to look into my own plate.

Because Black let me get near her, I thought, well let's take a closer look then. I went very near her, and, gee, she was annoyed with me. She started swearing and spitting but as she was doing so, she was still eating her food – she was really cute, swearing and eating.

I thought, well, she's only pretending to be tough, she isn't really, little miss beautiful. So I put my nose into her plate. I just wanted to have a sniff at the beef (as you know, I had my own plate if I wanted to eat some, but I thought my sister's was more interesting than mine). As I put my nose into Black's plate, the girl went berserk, she went mad at me. Gee, I've never seen miss beautiful so mad, man, I tell you!

As I was sniffing her beef she jumped on my neck, yeah, she did. She jumped on my neck and shoulder with shouts the like you've never heard before! She's ever so cute but when it comes to her grub, leave it alone! Gee, she scared the hell out of me. I never thought she'd be capable of such an outburst, just because I smelt her food.

Dad told me to back off. I didn't need telling, man. Such a beautiful Miss-Goody-Two-Shoes-Marilyn but then she goes mad in such a fashion. Man, I never imagined she could be

135

that tough. Dad got my little plate of beef and put it behind the plants in the front room, where I like having my meals, but I didn't touch it so dad went back to the kitchen and told mum, "Put a little gravy on his beef." So mum did just that, she put some gravy on my beef and dad brought it to me where I was sitting all alone in the front room. Delicious. "Kids!" said dad and he went back to the kitchen and told mum to remember to put gravy on my Sunday lunches from now on.

I'll write soonest, all the best,
Sir Norman

42. Someone wanted to steal my blanket

Good afternoon all,

I had a bit of a worry today because of my blanket. I think someone wanted to take it but I fought like a lion and I managed to keep it. Let me tell you all about it and how it happened.

You might recall from one of my letters, that I'd lost my dad for a few days some time ago, remember? Although I found dad after a few days, the whole episode got me really concerned. I thought, what if it happens again? What if I lose my dad again? All this anxiety was a little overwhelming, so I thought and I thought and I decided to change my habits a bit just to exert a little more control over my dad's whereabouts.

I used to spend lots of time sleeping on my dad's jumpers inside the wardrobe. I still do but much less than I used to. I decided instead (from a vast array of favourite places) to sleep in the upstairs corridor, just in front of my dad's study, so that I can keep an eye on him while I rest. That way, I can see every move he makes going in or out of his study, and so I shouldn't lose him ever again.

Although the corridor is quite warm because it's made of wood and there are some of mum's rugs, mum was worried that I wouldn't be warm enough sleeping in such an open area, so she decided to give me a blanket. It's folded several times so that it's thick and because it's wool it's very warm. I was very grateful and I made good use of it. I use it every day when I have my nap, usually in the afternoon.

137

The other night my sister Pirate wanted to borrow my blanket. Fair enough. I was sleeping on my armchair downstairs, so Pirate was welcome to sleep on the blanket upstairs, but the old girl had to be sick, didn't she! She couldn't be sick near it or better yet somewhere else entirely. No, no, not my sister Pirate, she had to be sick on my blanket. She didn't mean it, I know that, but nevertheless she could've made the effort to be sick somewhere else! Mum of course put the blanket in the washing machine and then outside on the clothes hoist to dry.

I happened to be outside as well with my dear sister Black Gold. I could see this blanket moving in all directions but as I was busy playing with Black, I was paying more attention to her than to the blanket. However, now and again I was looking at it out of the corner of my eye; you can't be too careful these days!

While I was playing and running around in the garden with Black Gold, I noticed that my blanket was moving differently. I carried on playing but I was getting more and more concerned about my blanket on the line. "It moved in a weird way again, I saw it," I said to Black Gold.

"Ppfffff," she said as usual.

I said, "Ppfffff? It's all very well for you to say that, it's not your blanket."

While I was talking to Black I could clearly see one corner of the blanket moving quite strangely and at that point I was majorly concerned so I decided to make a closer inspection. All of a sudden it did it again. Yeah, I definitely saw it this time, there had to be someone on the other side of the blanket trying to steal it. So I jumped on it, I jumped on it with all my might. I grabbed the corner with my front paws and I was absolutely determined not to let go. I managed to hang on for a while, but the flying blanket was so heavy that in the end I had to let go. But I stayed close by so that I could have another go as and when needed.

While I was lying flat on the grass, poised in a hunting position, the blanket flew oddly again so I didn't hesitate this time. I jumped again, and hurled myself with even more strength at the blanket. This time I managed to jump higher so that I could grab it with all four legs. And I wouldn't let it go, I just would not let go, I was determined to hang on. And while I was attached to the flying blanket, the wind blew so hard that I did an entire circuit on the line! Yeah, I did, I went all the way round, while I was hanging onto my blanket, I did, it's true!

I landed back on the grass, thoroughly puzzled by what had happened. I was bemused, I really was. I walked around the blanket but it was obvious there was no one on either side of it. I was a bit disappointed though because I'd wanted put up a fight and demonstrate my ability to defend my belongings.

Instead I decided to have a go at playing with my blanket. I took advantage of the wind blowing, hanging onto one side of the blanket as I was blown round and round on the line. All the while, Black Gold was running about on the opposite side of the blanket, trying to get at me while I was hanging onto it.

My dad thought it was the funniest thing he'd ever seen. He was watching the news on TV but when he saw all the enter-

tainment Black and I were creating in the garden, he switched
the TV off and watched us playing! I thought it was such fun
to be blown around like I was today so I rather hope mum
washes the blanket more often so that I can play with it like
that again! I'm no longer cross with Pirate for being sick on my
blanket, after all!

Will write soonest,
lots of love,
Sir Norman

43. There's a TV on

Hello, it's me again.

I discovered something funny. I thought it was one thing but it turns out it's something completely different and I can't wait to tell you all about it. My mum and dad laughed a lot and I'm sure you will too.

The other day I was in the kitchen. Obviously I've been there before but I must have been too busy to notice this thing.

After sitting there for a while I noticed something moving. The TV was switched on, I thought. The image wasn't very clear but it was definitely moving. I sat and watched it a bit longer to give myself more time to study this thing. I couldn't figure out for certain what it was. So I sat there, very still. I wasn't scared, just intrigued by this thing. It kept on moving and moving.

That's it, I thought, I think I know what it is, I've seen it in another room as well. I often watch it with dad in the sitting room. I knew what it was! A TV, I was sure it was a TV. Hmmm, yeah, yeah, a TV in the kitchen. It doesn't play any John Wayne movies though, and as I said, the image wasn't as clear as the other TV, and I couldn't really understand what they were saying.

I was sure it was a TV, but I wished someone would explain it to me. What bothered me was that, if I wanted to follow the image, my head had to go round and round, and sometimes it was going so fast that my head was spinning like a top. I

141

thought it was a TV that someone had been good enough to put low on the floor, so that I could watch it while I was sitting in the kitchen. But someone should fix the image, I thought, it's really blurred. And there are different colours, depending on the programme.

My dad's standing there with mum and he's laughing. Instead of standing there chuckling, I thought, couldn't you fix this thing? The image is rather bad, I can't say much for the sound either, can't you do something? I was sure it was a TV but the screen's round and so is the frame. So it was really rather intriguing; what could it be?

I heard my dad tell mum to make sure she always closes it properly. And I thought, what's the point of closing it? It's a TV, right? If so, why close it? I also heard my dad adding "We don't want Sir Norman going through the full programme, colour or heavy soiled white. All we need is for this kid to get trapped in the washing machine".

Well, I told you it was funny. I thought it was a TV but it turns out it's a washing machine! I still have so much to learn !

Much love,
Sir Norman

44. Short cut to self-service

Good afternoon everyone at Wild Berry,

This is urgent. I'm writing to you today because we need to discuss something between you, me and my mum and dad, and it's very urgent and important.

It's about my appetite. I have developed a huge appetite, I can eat like a small horse. I always finish all my food and my plates don't need to be washed because I lick them so clean that there's never a crumb left on them.

My mum's very worried about me putting on too much weight, in case it gives me trouble later on with my back legs. She worries a lot about this, so she controls how much she gives me to eat. My dad always says that I'm still growing and that I need more food to build up my bones and my muscles. I often hear dad saying to mum, "You're starving this poor kid." My dad's right, and I'm piggy in the middle because I want more food to eat!

I've learnt how to ask for food when my belly's really empty. I shout, I do pirouettes, I rush up and down where I have my meals, I make sure they know I'm hungry. My mum feeds me first in the morning for my breakfast. As a matter of fact, I make so much noise when she gets up that she has to feed me first, just to shut me up!

I also get fed at night, but twice a day isn't enough for me so, depending on how much my belly's rumbling, then I shout for more food either early evening, or just before going to bed. I can't bear the thought of mum going to bed without me having a bowl of biscuits, I really can't stand that at all. When my mum wants to be tough and doesn't feed me three times in a day, I get into a temper. I don't mean it but I'm so hungry that I really get into a rotten mood. I jump all over the place, on the dinner table, on the chairs, I also run around like a maniac. It's as if I can't control myself, my belly's empty and I just have to put food into it.

Today was one of these little episodes and although my dad was very amused, very, very amused, I wasn't that popular with mum.

What happened is that I slept almost all day. It was raining outside so I couldn't go out and play. I went to see where my sis Black was – she was upstairs on the landing so we stayed together for a little while and had a chat but then we decided to get some sleep, her on mum's table and me nearby on the chair. We slept for a while and then I heard Black getting up and I followed her. She went downstairs to see if the door was open so that we could go out, but it was still raining and we were confined to barracks.

All of a sudden my tummy was rumbling, really loud, I had one of these hunger attacks that I can't control. So I made some noise but I was ignored. I ran around the house, but again I was ignored and I started getting really annoyed. No one was paying me any attention. Mum was upstairs working on her computer, dad was watching the news and no matter what I did no one gave a toss about me. Black Gold went back upstairs. She has more experience that me and I'm sure she knew I was going to get into trouble, so she chickened out and left me.

So I decided to take action. You'll never guess what I did! Mum had grilled some sausages for dad's sandwiches and they were left on the stove to cool. I'd smelt something good cooking earlier but I got caught up in my own affairs. Now that I was so hungry, though, I decided to take a closer look. I had to be careful not to get caught so I had to be crafty. From the sitting room, there's something like a window in the wall. This thing had often intrigued me quite a bit in the past so now I tried to lift myself up so I could investigate it with my front paws to see where it leads to. I discovered it leads to the kitchen and although it's a bit complicated, I figured with some skilful jumping I could probably make it. Action for food!

As I said, my dad was watching TV on the sofa. I jumped onto the sofa, from the sofa I jumped onto the coffee table, from the coffee table I jumped onto the edge of this little window in the wall. The whole thing took me less than a second. I never missed any of the gaps in between the sofa and the table, the table and the wall. Speed conquers everything!

Once I was on the edge of this window, I had to go across a kitchen counter where mum keeps a fruit basket, and all the jars with our biscuits. Hmmm, tempting, but she keeps them all sealed, so I couldn't help myself to any biscuits. From there I jumped onto the kitchen table. It's what humans call a gateleg table which sounds impressive but what I discovered is that jumping on it really makes a huge amount of noise because of the wooden flap. From the table I jumped onto a chair and from the chair onto the stove where I got myself a sausage! Yeah, man, I did, you heard it right, I nicked a sausage! I was so starved! I thought it wouldn't be quite right to eat from the plate on the stove, so I took the sausage to the floor and started eating it. That's when mum found me. Mum heard all the kerfuffle from upstairs. It was the kitchen table that gave me away, it was so noisy. Mum not only found me in the kitchen eating sausages but she also found dad laughing like mad because he'd watched the whole episode.

I looked my mum straight in the eye with one of my paws on the sausage! Dad said that my look was saying, "I was so hungry that I took a short cut to self-service." That's exactly what I meant. For once, mum didn't know what to say! She took my sausage, broke it into smaller pieces and gave them to me in a bowl. That was a good snack!

So dad suggested I have a word with you so that you can tell mum to feed me more. Can you please do so? Many thanks.

The episode didn't quite end here as my dad got a bit of an ear bashing (don't say I told you). I heard mum and dad talking a little later. Dad was trying to explain to her what he's already said many times, that I need more food. But mum is rather strict on this point and she says I've grown so much that all of you at Wild Berry won't recognise me at all next time you see me. Dad says it's only normal because I'm growing well but mum doesn't want to hear.

But then dad said to my mum, "Really, we have to give it to him."

"To whom?" mum replied.

"Good old Nico," dad said.

"What do you mean, *good old Nico?*" said mum.

146

"Yeah, he's really talented, he did a terrific job on him." By 'him' he meant little old me!

Dad added, "Look at all the trouble Sir Norman went to get himself into the kitchen. If it hadn't been for Nico doing that great job on him, he'd never have been able to do that." Mum had a go at dad for calling Nico *old*. She asked dad whether he'd looked at himself in the mirror lately, that was the first point! And the second point mum had a go about was the fact that of course Nico was wonderful for having operated on me so successfully, but that didn't mean dad could just let me misbehave. He'd been downstairs and could've prevented me from performing all those daredevil stunts all over the place! Dad's always in trouble for something or another.

Will write soon again, much love,
Sir Norman

45. Black Gold has had an operation

Dear friends,

Thank you for looking after my sis Black Gold. As you know, Black has come back home now. I'm really happy about her coming home, she's now my best friend and I missed her very much. You don't realise how very beautiful and thick her fur is until Nico gives her one of his Mohican cuts. Gee, that guy will never make it in a lady's hair salon. Before she had the operation, Black lost an awful lot of weight, which isn't a bad thing really, but the point is that she'd really lost a lot, so when Nico shaved her neck for the operation, there was almost only skin and bones left; scary sight!

When she came home from the surgery, of course the first thing she wanted to do was eat. She always gets starved when she goes for a car drive, so this poor girl came home and went straight to the kitchen for food. She looked so tiny without her fur. One of her legs was shaved as well, it looked just like a cheese stick, only the wrong colour. But the most impressive was her neck. Her neck without fur was really impressive; long, tiny, pink, skinny, terribly skinny, and with several stitches.

My dad, well you know how he is, he put his foot in it again! Black Gold had only been home a short while when dad inspected her. He kept asking, "What do you look like?" Over and over he kept asking this. Dad was sitting in his armchair thinking, then all of a sudden he calls us all around, and then in a very solemn voice he declared, "I know what she looks like." We all waited anxiously. "She looks like a turkey that

148

missed the chop." Needless to say, mum was outraged! Comparing her little princess to a turkey! To this day I believe that Black understood what dad said because she isn't on very good terms with him!

All the best now, will write again soonest,
Sir Norman

46. I get it from Johnny Weissmuller

My dear friends,

I believe I might be in a little trouble but, as usual, I'm not too worried about it, I should be able to get away with it.

As you're well aware from my letters, I'm a little bit of a 'walking disaster' as mum puts it. But my other passion is climbing. I just love it! I climb as high as I possibly can. The thing is that, although I personally find it very amusing, it doesn't always fit in with my life in a civilised society.

I discovered a new game! I run all over the house, then I go upstairs, I jump on the bed, then straight onto one of the bedside cabinets, then onto the window sill and run along it! It's very challenging and extremely funny!

I like this stunt because it always impresses the birds! They sit singing all day long on the edge of the roof just above the bedroom. Mum always keeps the fanlight open, and sometimes she used to keep the main window open too, but since she's seen what I'm capable of, she's been worried the next stunt I pulled would be jumping straight out of the window, so she now makes sure the window is always closed!

The stunt itself is rather audacious but I was never scared simply because I knew that if I missed, I'd still have both the curtains and the nets to grab hold of. I know, it's not conventional behaviour but you have to adapt, don't you think? And this morning I did just that! I was running like a mad hatter all over the place. I was tremendously bored because it was early morning and everybody was asleep. I can never understand why it is that I'm left alone and no one wants to play with me at 5.00am. I have no alternative but to entertain myself so, here I was, running around. I even ran over my mum and dad as they slept; as I said, it was very early morning.

I jumped onto the bedside cabinet and then onto the window sill. But I think I was being a little over-zealous ... and I missed! There was dead silence, neither mum nor dad said a word. I guess they were waiting for the big crash, but it didn't happen!

Mum and dad were both sitting on the bed by now, but still not talking. Silence. Nothing was happening and I could hear dad asking mum, "Where on earth did he finish up?" Mum got up and I could hear and feel her moving about from where I was. She looked here and there.

"Can you see him?" asked dad.

"No," replied mum.

"Open the curtain," said dad.

She did and I was found – hanging! With one front leg I was hanging from the nets, with the other front leg I hung from the curtains. When mum opened the curtains carefully I was completely exposed with my belly on full display. Since I no longer have my credentials at least I was decent!

As usual in such cases, mum rescued me with a cuddle. Dad wasn't too impressed with my audacity, though, and grumbled a bit, hoping to get back to sleep. He said I must have been watching Arnie videos! He got it all wrong, my dad. I don't want to go into politics, so I don't watch Arnie, I prefer watching Tarzan. Jumping and climbing all over the rainforest, it's so much more fun to watch than boring old Arnie and all the women going hysterical about him.

When it was a decent time to get up, dad took a look at the window, just to make sure everything was in order. It wasn't! I'd managed to bend the steel rod for the nets on one side. Dad was less than impressed! "I'll give him Tarzan," he said. I had to make an effort to keep a low profile for a little while, just to keep out of my dad's sight for the morning. You know what I mean, don't you?!

Bye for now,
Sir Norman

47. Christmas lunch

Hello everyone,

Hope all is well with you and that you had a Christmas as nice as mine! It was my very first taste of end-of-year festivities, not only in my house but with human beings and with my sisters. I'm convinced that my dear sister Black Gold was royalty in a previous life! My admiration for her has no limits, not only is she beautiful but she is so well groomed and behaves in such a manner that no one can equal her in any way.

Mum cooked an enormous bird in the oven! It was e-n-o-r-m-o-u-s! I have never seen such a big bird in my life. Everything happened so quickly and I was so caught up in my own affairs that I didn't see how it got into the house and how it managed to lose all its feathers. Because of its size, it must have taken quite a bit to clean it up. I looked everywhere but I couldn't spot a feather anywhere. I was intrigued.

While I had so many questions about this huge bird going round in my head, my two sisters appeared in the kitchen while mum was preparing it. Their eyes were open wide and bigger than I'd ever seen them! It was obvious to me that they were familiar with such a big thing. Then my dad turned up in the kitchen too and they were all talking about this beauty in the roasting pan, and I was still trying to figure out what it was.

A turkey, I was told. This bird is called a turkey. Man, it must have been ten times as big as me! What on earth are we going to do with such a big turkey, I wondered. And I also wondered if dad had invited the army for lunch, but on second thoughts, and seeing how my sisters were reacting to the whole thing, I preferred to think that we were going to have a feast!

Christmas day arrived and this turkey looked fabulous! Mum brought it to the table and it was dad's duty to slice it. One of mum's friends was spending the day with us, and we were all gathered around the table, waiting for dad to get on with his cutting duties.

I couldn't rest, nor could my sisters! We could see the plates being brought to the table and then, lucky us, we heard the clatter of our own little plates. My sisters went spare, they couldn't stand still if they'd tried! Usually we take our meals in the kitchen but on this occasion the plates were brought to the dining room, so there was a little confusion to say the least.

I've told you before, Black Gold has huge eyes and waiting for her Christmas lunch, they were even bigger, they looked like saucers! Dad cut the turkey and served everyone, then, oh bliss, we could hear that something was happening with our plates. Meat was put in them and mum was cutting those wonderful slices into rough smaller pieces and we got served. I thought all my Christmases had come at once. Well, it *was* Christmas, after all!

As I said earlier, I think my sis Black must have been royalty in her previous life, and before anyone had a chance to give us our plates, she jumped up onto one of the chairs around the dinner table. Naturally, us four-legged creatures are spoilt but even so, we've never been allowed to walk on the table while there's food on it. (I personally like to stretch on it when the sun is shining through the window though.) Anyway, Black Gold was by then on the chair next to our guest, and the lady very kindly went to take Black Gold's plate and put it on the floor for her. She never got the chance. As the lady took the plate from the table and showed it to Black, intending to put it on the floor, Black Gold stretched out one of her arms, took a piece of turkey with her paw and started eating it on the chair. The lady was quite uncomfortable because the chairs are covered with a light-coloured velvet fabric – oooops! The only thing this lady could do was sit at the table with her own food waiting on her plate, holding Black Gold's plate in her hands.

Dad intervened and said, "Don't worry about the chair, just put Black's plate on the chair and let her enjoy herself, before she jumps onto the table and starts helping herself to your dinner." Of course everyone laughed and the lady did just that, she put Black's plate on the chair and everyone was happy.

I turned my plate around, I was so excited with the whole thing. My sisters had already finished their turkey so I hurried to eat mine, just in case one of them decided to come and see if I needed any help, and eventually I finished mine too. I could hear that everyone was getting animated and was laughing around the table. You want to know what Black Gold did then?

She wanted some more turkey and in no time at all and before anyone could say a word, she sat on the chair properly and put her two front paws on the table. Her paws are magnificent, very large and with white gloves, exquisitely elegant. Her neck was stretched to the maximum, her eyes were even larger than usual, and as she sat there like royalty she was scanning everything on the table with a particular focus on the large serving plate where the turkey was looking majestic.

Everyone was amazed by her behaviour, and dad cut some more meat for her. The whole time, she sat there waiting with her front paws glued to the dinner table. Dad said, "That's my girl. You can take her anywhere and be proud of her."

I must admit, she was really cute at the dinner table!

Lots of love,
Sir Norman

48. I think a LearJet is trying to land in our garden

Hello my friends,

I got worried about something that occurred the other day
and I wanted to tell you all about it, in case it comes to your
garden; I wanted to warn you.

I was in the garden one day doing my daily John Wayne patrol
duties. There are so many bushes and several trees so I'm
quite busy all the time now, and as I was patrolling, mum was
watching me from the kitchen window. Because of my beloved household, I take my role very seriously and I take pride
in protecting everyone around me. I also count every single
bird and I keep a close eye on the doves. As I told you in one
of my letters, they particularly annoy me and one day I'm going to teach one of them a good lesson.

Anyway, back to my patrolling. There was this thing circling
around in the sky above our house and garden. It flew over
once, twice, then it disappeared, then flew back even closer to
the ground. Gee it was impressive!

I've seen a lot of programmes on the telly lately about planes
and fighter planes, you know, with everything going on these
days, and although I'd never seen such a thing flying in the sky
above my garden before, I couldn't help but think it was a
plane, a small one but still a plane!

The fuselage was sleek and elegant, the nose was pointed like a
Concorde, but I said to myself, Concorde, I've seen on the
news, isn't flying any more, so surely it can't come to my gar-

den, can it? It was obvious that this thing knew exactly what it was doing, and that made me think that it must have had a good GPS navigation system to be able to manoeuvre so well.

It was rather small but when it deployed the wings, then gee, it wasn't that small after all. Gosh, I thought, I wonder whose toy this is. Never mind who it belongs to, if this thing comes down any closer to my garden, I'm going to catch it and make it land. It was flying above me, once to the right, then to the left. Where's it gone now? Oh, it's behind me now, good flying. My mum was still at the kitchen window and by then dad was with her and I could see them looking at me with a very amused expression on their faces.

All of a sudden, this thing made a majestic landing on top of the silver birch, "Oh dear", I thought, "maybe it's in trouble." I didn't know that planes could land on a tree branch, did you? Maybe it's having mechanical problems, I thought. I looked at my dad, he was standing on the kitchen steps. I looked at the plane, looked back at dad.

"It's next door's heron," I heard him say to mum.

Oh, well, I still have so many things to learn! If it happens to fly your way, don't be alarmed, it's not sent by the intelligence agencies to spy on you. It's circling for a chance to get a fish from the pond next door, and then it flies off for some exercise! Truly!

I'll let you know if I see it again.

All the best,
Sir Norman

49. My pink nose was almost blue

Hello, it's me,

Gosh, I almost went through the glass door this morning. You know I told you that I'm training hard to hunt birds, right? Well, this morning I spent a lot of time outside doing so, then it started raining and I had to retreat inside. Mum and dad were watching the midday news on the TV and I was with them, but instead of watching the news, I was keeping an eye on the birds outside. You have no idea how unkind they are to me. When I'm outside they stay away from me and I have to work hard chasing them, but as soon as I come indoors they all seem to organise a convention on my patio, and they arrive in hundreds!

I was in the sitting room on the other side of the sliding doors. I keep track of all these birds so my head was going madly from side to side, just trying to keep up with these little creatures. They never stop moving and so it's a lot of hard work for me to count them. They're everywhere, on the patio, on the outside table, on the washing lines. They even dare to come to the water bowl on the patio, I tell you they've got some nerve!

So I was busy looking all around and all of a sudden a little robin was on the steps of our sitting room. Gosh, he was little but ever so fat! He was so round and plump, and it was just getting to my snack time. I know my mum would say he was ever so cute but, hey, I am what I am and to me he just looked appetising. He was just a few inches away from me, such a temptation! So I thought no more about what mum would say and wallop, I jumped at him! I made such a noise, such a noise, and I saw quite a few little stars going around in my head, and there were birds singing as well.

Mum and dad stopped watching the TV and, amongst the stars going around, I could see mum and dad's faces coming quite close. Mum asked dad, "Do you think he hurt himself?" Dad looked at me and replied, "I think he might just remember this one."

Oh, golly, I tell you, I forgot the glass sliding door was between the robin and me.

Bye for now from a little bruised
Sir Norman

50. They are going to patent my paws

Yo, it's me,

How are you today? You know by now that I'm naughty, right? I like challenges! I'm very well fed here but this doesn't stop me being naughty!

I just like the buzz that I get from stealing things. Well, not things really, my dad's dinner in particular, ha, ha, ha! I've got the hang now of how to open the packaging and without noise, or almost!

Now, I'll tell you my secret!

If it's cling film, I just use one of my claws. I open my paw wide and extend the claw, and this allows me to slide the film off without any problem at all. If it's foil, that's a little more complicated because whatever you do, it's noisy! But even so, I can manage quite easily; I just use both my paws. I make a small hole in the foil with one of my claws and then with both paws I push the foil to either side to make a bigger hole.

Can you picture the scene? If not, let me know and I'll demonstrate.

Once I've dealt with the packaging, I help myself to whatever is inside. Most of the time it's either sliced beef or pork, and I like both. Mum said the other day that my paws and claws need patenting, whatever that means!
Speak to you soonest,
Sir Norman

51. Teamwork

Hello there,

Just a little note to let you know that the three of us were caught in the act today. No worries! We got away with it. Now, on behalf of Pi and Black and myself, I'm going to tell you all about it!

I've told you before that I love sausages, remember? Well, my sisters like sausages too! So now that we've found out that we have this little thing in common, we had a meeting between the three of us and we reached a consensus. When mum leaves the sausages on the stove, whoever sees them tells the other two and organises an expedition. As a matter of fact it just happened. And even now, neither mum nor dad know who carried out the raid. All they know is that it can only be either me or Black because Pirate doesn't do such things, she just commands others to do them for her. So I won't tell you who did it, me or Black.

We were caught, the three of us, on the kitchen floor, making a feast out of a sausage. The three of us were very busy, eating the same sausage! It was a lot of fun and we didn't even argue! We didn't even lift our little heads up to look at mum when she arrived, we only did that when just crumbs were left on the floor. And as I told you, we didn't get told off. What can they do? Nothing!

Speak soon, much love,
Sir Norman

52. Lunch sandwiches

Hello dear all,

I just wanted to let you know that I'm OK, you don't need to worry about me. I'm very well treated here and if I were to want for anything I know how ask for it.

Over the Christmas period there were all sorts of things to eat. I mean, not really for us four-legged creatures, but for mum and dad and their guests. Stuff that I'd never seen before, funny-shaped biscuits, stinking cheese, you name it.

There was one particular thing they were eating that I was especially curious about. The packaging was rather bulky and the stuff inside was pinkish-orange! Just the colour intrigued me, surely these folks can't eat this stuff, can they? I don't believe this.

When mum opened the packaging, holy mackerel, did it smell, not only was it orange, but the smell was worse than all the repellent I've ever come across in my life! Having said that, I could see my big sis Pirate getting really agitated; she'd come out of nowhere to see what was going on.

She was trying to stretch herself up to the table top where mum was dealing with this thing. I couldn't believe that Pirate, such high society that she is, could be interested in this horrible smelly stuff. Then on second thoughts, I said to myself, my sis Pi is really very well behaved, she knows a thing or two, she's been around, surely she must know something, right? If she's after this stuff, it must be something good. So I asked her, "Hey, big sis, what is that stuff?" The look I got! OK, she might be nicknamed the Queen Bee but, gee, she doesn't need to be that snooty with me, does she?

"Well, don't give me that look, sis, I've never seen the stuff before," I said. "What do you use this for? Surely it can't be eaten, can it? It smells so bad." My sis was really not impressed with me but she kept shouting at mum to give her some.

"Hey, sis, don't be like that, tell me what it is."

Pirate answered back, "It's smoked salmon, you dope."

Gee, smoked salmon. I'd had some salmon before, out of a tin, but smoked salmon? Anyway, while all these thoughts were going round in my head, I could see mum giving a good dollop of the stuff to Pirate! Apparently, I was told, Pirate is mad about it, she'd go a long way to get some and every year for Xmas, as a treat, mum saves some for her! As I was in the kitchen, I was given a small piece in my plate but I wasn't too keen on it. I ate it anyway but it took me a while.

After this little episode I was intrigued and as I follow Pirate about quite a lot these days (let me rephrase that, Pirate is good enough to *allow* me to follow her), I said to myself, she's so posh, my sis, that I've got to get to eat more like her.

A few days after this happened, I was outside in the garden minding my own business and mum was making sandwiches. Mum got the smoked salmon out of the fridge and she was about to use some. I was told afterwards that both Pi and Black came out of nowhere and wanted some. So out come two little plates with some of the stuff on it for my sisters and they had a snack. In the meantime I came back in from the garden and I saw Pirate licking her chops like crazy! I was about to ask her what she'd had but the smell was so strong that I didn't need to, I knew immediately what she'd eaten. I parked myself in the middle of the kitchen and I yelled my head off. Truly, I did, I shouted with all the strength my lungs would permit!

Mum came back into the kitchen in no time! She asked, "What on earth do you want, shouting so loud?" I made mum understand that I wanted to see her sandwich, no kidding, I stared at mum's sandwich from the floor!

Mum said, "You don't like it."

"What do you mean I don't like it?"

And mum said again, "I didn't call you for any because you had some the other day and you didn't like it."

Now, with all due respect if you please, may I be allowed to take decisions by myself? My little person is quite capable of making decisions, and I'm the one who decides whether or not I like some stuff or not. While I was trying to make mum understand that I was appalled that she should make decisions for me, I rushed to the front room, jumped through the serving hatch, stood on the top where my eating place is, and shouted some more!

By then dad turned up to see for himself what all the kerfuffle was about and mum was trying to explain to him that I didn't like smoked salmon. And as she was saying that she put her sandwich close to my nose so that she could prove to dad what she was saying was true. As I smelt the salmon, my moustache curled even more! I shouted again. Dad laughed and said to mum, "I'm not sure your theory's right, give him a small piece and see what he does." So mum obliged. And of course I had to prove her wrong, I swallowed the salmon in no time and shouted for some more! So mum gave me the salmon from her own sandwich. I love the stuff now, my sis Pi won't look down on me any more about this one!

Yes, you guessed it, mum ended up having buttered bread, while I had the salmon!

Much love from
Sir Norman

53. I did it; I couldn't put up with it any longer, so I attacked it

Hello all,

I just wanted to inform you that I couldn't face its inactivity any longer, so I attacked it. I'm going to tell you what happened.

It's been bothering me ever since I arrived here. Truly, since the very early days! This thing is moved from one room to another depending on how mum needs to use it. It's rather pretentious, very often you can see it looking at itself in the mirror. It doesn't speak, doesn't joke, it's not nice. I know I'm the latest one to move in here so I have to make an effort to fit in with the others but this one I just can't be friends with. I've tried several times to speak to it. I sit there and stare at it. I move my head from side to side to see whether it'd follow my movements; it doesn't.

I'd been thinking about doing this for quite a while. I was caught a few times standing on the tallboy cabinet trying to reach this stupid creature, but every time mum warned me not to fall off the cabinet. I'm telling you, I want to give it a good hiding, never mind falling off the cabinet.

I tried everything to make it talk to me, without success. It's just there, it doesn't smile or speak, doesn't move, never says a word, never, just stands there like a stupid twit. I never said anything about my frustration to my sisters, as I was planning on giving it a good hiding and I was a little concerned that if I said anything to my sisters one or the other would have said something, and tried to stop me. So the other morning, I went for it. Mum was in one room and this Mr. Zomby-thing was in the other room. I jumped onto the tallboy cabinet and then whammmmmmmmm, I leapt at it! My mum's eyes were bigger than Black Gold's, for in no time she was standing in the doorway of the room, her mouth wide open. I never realised I could impress mum that much.

I had my two front legs gripping onto it as well as one of my back legs. The second back leg was trying to keep my balance on the cabinet; it was quite an acrobatic pose to say the least! It was a jolly good thing this creature was covered in cloth so that I could get a good grip on it, otherwise I don't know how or where I would have ended up.

The thing is that, in the process of attacking this stupid thing, quite a few decorative bits and pieces from the top of the cabinet were now on the floor … ooooops! Yeah, I admit I created quite a bit of noise in the process, but guess what? This thing never even moved, or tried to defend itself, nothing!

Mum wasn't that impressed. She didn't have a go at me but I knew she wasn't impressed. In the process of me playing the acrobat, I damaged the cloth covering this stupid creature. Well, you know, I didn't mean it, but whenever my claws get hold of something it tends to leave my signature, and I had to grab hold of something! You know what? Even after the attack this thing had no fear!

I just couldn't make it move. I remained perplexed! Gee, this is a tough one, tougher than I thought! My dad came home a little later and when he saw mum I heard him saying, "Something tells me that something happened." I was keeping a low profile curled up in the armchair. I then heard mum telling dad that I attacked the sewing stand. Oh, I thought it was a person! Now I understand why it wasn't friendly!

Speak to you soonest,
Sir Norman

54. The eggs business

Good afternoon,

I'm just writing you a note to inform you that if you're looking for me, I'm hiding somewhere in the garden, I'm not
flavour of the day today. What happened is, I'm still discover-
ing plenty of new things and I get so excited, I get over-
whelmed and then of course I get into trouble.

This morning mum went to the farm to get some eggs and
she came back with a tray. She called my dad and I heard her
saying to him that because the eggs were so fresh, he could
have scrambled eggs for lunch and he agreed. I didn't really
know what mum was talking about but I heard her in the
kitchen, and that was enough to convince me that there was
likely to be some food production, and that maybe, in the heat
of it all, I might get something nice.

So I jumped onto the kitchen worktop and I watched my
mum beating the eggs while dad looked on from a distance.
Mum put the bowl with the eggs on one side while she
opened the cupboard door to get the pepper. As she did so, I
smelt the eggs and had a go, I tried some; not bad. As I was
licking my chops, mum could hear dad laughing, she turned
round and saw me with my head deep in the bowl.

She told me to get out of there and then turned to dad asking, "What do I do now?" My dad's always very pragmatic,
even more so when he's hungry and waiting for his food, so
he responded, "Put it in the frying pan and cook it, woman."
Yeah, that was his reply! And that was that, he had his long-

awaited scrambled eggs. But that wasn't the end of it. Mum went to do some other things upstairs and left the egg tray on the kitchen top.

Now, you know that I'm really passionate about football. I often play with the fruit basket on the other kitchen counter. I get a mandarin or a lemon or a kiwi out of the basket, or now and again I also nick a small potato or a small onion from the vegetable basket under the kitchen counter, and then I punch whatever I nicked with my front paw and play football with it. It's a good game, I enjoy it.

The thing is that today I played that game with an egg, and not a hard-boiled egg either, no, no, no, a fresh egg I took from the tray. It rolled quite well on the kitchen top. Yeah, I was having a good time.

Yeah, I know now that it was the wrong thing to do! I smashed the egg. I mean I didn't smash it, exactly, it just rolled too far and too fast, and smashed itself against the corner of the sink. Oooops. Yep, you could say that. I wasn't aware that breaking things makes a mess! That yukky transparent stuff coming out of the egg went everywhere on the counter and then took a turn and started dripping all down the washing machine and onto the floor. What a mess!

Mum came back into the kitchen when she heard dad saying to me, "You're gonna be in trouble, mate." When mum appeared in the kitchen she had one of those looks on her face. I looked at dad and said to myself, "Oh, oh, I think I can see trouble."

Dad gave me very sound advice, "If I were you, mate, I'd go

171

out to catch birds for a little while, when she's got that look on her face, it's the best course of action." He didn't need to tell me twice, I went off as quickly as I could. Having given me that sound advice, and before I could reach the exit through the flap, I heard dad walking away from the kitchen singing that song, "I think I see a pussy cat a-creeping up on me."

Now you know, if you're looking for me, I'm hiding in the garden.

Speak soon,
Sir Norman

55. Today I went on hunger strike

Yeah, truly I did! Good morning all.

I did, for two minutes, that is. Listen to this. I've learnt in the past few months since my official entry into society, that if people care they will do lots and lots for you, if they don't care then forget it, you're just wasting your time. But if they do care, then go for it!

Spoilt, that's the word, I'm spoilt, I know, but then why not take advantage of it? My sisters do, why shouldn't I?

I like my food very much. I enjoy as much as I can get and mum feeds me with the various sachets she finds in the shops. I get quite a variety of it; fish, meat, super-meat, fish mixed with prawns, you name it.

My sisters don't like sachets, just one brand called HiLife. They would, wouldn't they, HiLife food! But in the morning, they have special food for their breakfast. I have one of those sachets but they have tuna from a tin mixed up with either wet food or biscuits from the special range that Black Gold needs. Recently, I've been taking a closer look at their breakfast but, as I'm scared to miss out, I always shove my nose deep back into my own bowl of food. A couple of weeks ago mum tried me with some of the same breakfast as my sisters but I was spoilt for choice and I couldn't make up my mind, so she continued to feed me my sachets.

I thought about it and thought about it and, as my sis Pi and me are getting closer and closer and I admire her very much,

173

it occurred to me that Pi knows what life is all about, so I should copy her and follow her example.

A couple of mornings mum noticed that I was slow eating my breakfast, taking longer than usual to eat, but she just thought I wasn't that hungry. That wasn't the case, actually I wanted to make her understand that I wanted the same breakfast as my sisters, but how can a cat make a human being understand quickly? How can I make mum understand what I want? So this morning, when I was served breakfast, I smelt the food in my bowl but didn't touch it. This was tough because it smelt pretty good but I want to be like my sisters. Mum couldn't comprehend my meaning at first so she got a fork out of the drawer to cut my food into smaller pieces. That didn't work. She then stirred the food around, but that didn't work either. I was getting impatient because I was getting really hungry. What could I do? I continued to sit next to my bowl but didn't touch the food.

Then all of a sudden, I had an idea. I went to the edge of the kitchen counter and looked down on my sister Black Gold! Mum got the message, at last! She asked me if I wanted the same food as my sisters. At last! She understood. She prepared a little bowl of food as she would do for my sisters, gave it to me, and I ate the lot! Mum couldn't believe it!

I heard her talking to dad and explaining to him that I went on hunger strike. I was ever so pleased that I'd managed to impress the family! Ever since, I now get my breakfast in the morning like my sisters and I'm very pleased about it.

Much love,
Sir Norman

56. What kind of creature is that?

Good morning all,

I wanted to share with you my thoughts about some creature that lives in the garden next to mine.

Have you guys ever taken the time to sit down and look at a poodle? I mean, one's got to have some guts to go out with a coat like a poodle's. I've lived here for a few months now, and that dog next door never ceases to grab my attention! I spend hours in my garden looking at him, I should say staring at him, but to this day I can't comprehend why such a creature exists!

That dog keeps on barking. That in itself would be pretty annoying, barking! For what? Not only does he bark but he's got such a voice. Anyone in their right mind would take voice coaching just to get rid of that silly voice of his!

The other day, I just had to call him over nearer to the fence and ask him, "Please enlighten me", I said. "If, and I say if, you had the chance to get hold of me, would you eat me alive?" Mr. Poodle looked at me, and of course he is far from bright, so he couldn't say a thing, could he?!

I repeated my question, "If you just had the remotest chance of getting one of your paws on me, then what would you do? Eat me alive?" He couldn't answer. There he was looking at me with a silly face, his mouth open ready to bark again but certainly no guts for action!

"There you are," I said. "All bark and no action, so just zip it and stop barking!" He was still standing there, looking silly with his two ears on each side of his face. "What do you look like, man?" I asked. "Can't you see yourself in the mirror? Why don't you do

175

something about yourself? Look at the way your fur is trimmed, how can you go out looking like that?"

I'm sure I was annoying him but, to be honest, that was my intention. I can't stand the guy, he barks all the time at everything. He just has to see a bird and he barks, and as we've got hundreds of birds in the garden, I'll let you do the mathematics. He sees a fly, he barks. He hears the milkman, he barks, the postman, you name it, he never shuts up! Then he stands there on the other side of the fence, as if he'd like to jump over onto our side and attack us, so I conferred with my sisters and I decided to ask him directly what his intentions were. My sister Black Gold thinks she's so beautiful that she's got no time for him. For once, I agree with her, she would be wasting her time if she were to even glance at him!

My sister Pirate is just like me, she can't stand him, she thinks he's really silly. She too stands on our side of the garden and looks at him asking herself, "What does this creature look like?" Now that Pi and I are buddies, we both spend time looking at him and then we tell him, "Just you come over here, then you'll see what we're capable of."

Mr. Poodle was trying to say something, but before he could pronounce a word I said to him, "Look mate, don't even bother. If you want a fight, you come over, if not then zip it and mind your own business."

Since I had a go at him, he's been a bit better. But I honestly think he has the brain of a frozen pea, so it won't be long before one of us has another go at him. After this little episode Pi and I sat down and exchanged our views on him and we both agreed that he might want to give us the impression that he's very posh but he's not. He's just a normal dog with an expensive coat. Don't you agree with us? Much love,

Sir Norman

57. Close encounter

Hello to everyone,

I just wanted to send you a little note to inform you about something funny that happened with my sister Pirate! At first I really didn't think it was that funny because I felt a little squashed to say the least, but then I saw the funny side of it.

Both Pi and I spend lots of time together. She's still a bit of a Queen Bee but, as long as I keep on her good side, I like the old girl very much and she teaches me lots of good tricks, so I follow her as much as I can. To be absolutely honest, we're now quite inseparable, not just buddies!

On Sunday we were both in the garden. Actually my sister Black Gold was with us too and we had a great time together. We jumped up and down, and we ran after each other. We work as a team trying to catch some bird or another, we tease Mr. Poodle next door. I mean, you know, we have a good time together.

I think I've already told you, they're doing some engineering work on the railway in some villages further down from where we live, so from time to time there are some big machines that come down on the railway. They're big machines, real big, even you would be scared, I tell you! Really, even you would be scared!

So, Sunday we played in the garden. Everything was very quiet because there are no trains on a Sunday. Black Gold was playing with us but, as she's such a proper lady, she doesn't get messy like Pi and me, so she wasn't as engrossed as we were. All of a sudden, we saw her run like an arrow towards the kitchen! Pi and I looked at each other. "What on earth did she see?" we asked each other.

By then Black was right back in the kitchen, with mum preparing the Sunday lunch. All of a sudden, there was this mighty noise coming out of nowhere. It was like a huge fan blowing down our way, I'd never heard such a noise! As it approached the back of our garden we could see a huge machine. To say 'huge' is an understatement, the thing was colossal, I tell you, colossal.

Pi and I both ran for our lives towards the kitchen door. We both arrived at the same time so can you guess what happened next? Go on, have a guess.

We both went through the cat flap at the same time. Mum heard a commotion at the door, she immediately put the knife and the veggies that she was preparing down on the table top and came towards us. I guess she just wanted to release us, as we were stuck half-way through the flap. Both our heads and shoulders went through but the rest of us remained outside!

It all happened in a matter of seconds! By the time mum got near the door, it felt as if the colossal ugly machine was just behind us, so we pushed like mad through the flap and managed to get into the kitchen!

As I told you, no one in this house is allowed to say that Pirate is a fat girl; that means trouble with dad! So I won't say that my sis is fat, she's just pleasantly plump and her plumpness made my close encounter with her a matter of life and death.

178

By the way, I'm not sure I mentioned that our flap isn't a cat flap, it's a dog flap! But we still got stuck in it. Dad asked mum whether she thought she was drunk, seeing one cat with two heads and four front legs!

I got a fright, I tell you! Gee, we both got a fright and Pi didn't even remember to spit at me because I was too close!

I'll keep you informed what happens next!

Best thoughts,
Sir Norman

58. Black Gold told me she saw a bizarre creature

Hello to you all,

This morning Black came to see you all for a routine check-up with Dr. Nik and she had plenty to tell me when she got back!

She said that once she arrived at Wild Berry, there were plenty of people as usual. Naturally, as ever, she didn't forget to tell me that she got lots of compliments from everyone! I know she's very pretty and because she doesn't like being shut up in a basket, mum takes her in the car and, once she arrives, everyone talks to her and cuddles her because she socialises with everyone. It's as simple as that!

Anyway, I'm now getting used to her goody-two-shoes attitude, so she told me that Mrs. A told her this, and Mrs. B told her that, and Mr. Z said this, and Miss X that, etc., you know women, when they start telling you about their outings.

All of a sudden a lady came out of Dr. Nik's consultancy room with a basket that she put on the bench next to my sis. At first Black thought nothing of it, she said that she thought it was just another cat. Then the lady started talking to mum as they'd met before and, while the two of them were chatting, Black had a closer look inside the basket.

Black said that she tried talking to this creature but couldn't get any response. Every other four-legged creature in the waiting room had something to say but this one was silent. "What did you do", I asked my sis, "didn't you say something to him?"

"Well," she said, "I tried to start a conversation with him, as it was clear from the number of people there that we'd have to wait quite a bit. I put my nose right up close to his basket door but he remained unfazed!" I guess this got right up her nose; Black Gold, the Princess, no one ever ignores her, so I bet it annoyed her that this thing –whatever it was – wouldn't speak to her!

I asked Black Gold, "But did you know for sure it was a he and not a she?"

"Well, judging by his manners only a bloke could have been rude enough not to engage in conversation, a lady would have responded," said my sis. I had nothing to add to that, better to shut up.

I asked Black again, "But what did he look like, then?" I was by now very intrigued! She said it was like a cat, had four legs for sure but was shorter than a cat. Hummmm, the poor thing, I was thinking! She said the weird thing was that he had no moustache, she couldn't see a moustache like we have. I was getting more and more intrigued.

"Well," I said, "maybe someone shaved him and cut his moustache by mistake." My sister remained perplexed.

Then she said something that worried me. She said, "Don't tell anybody but this poor creature was like a cat but with very long ears." She spoke as if she was telling me her deepest darkest secret. Very long ears? That was spooky!
I asked her, "Well, did you ask him what happened with his ears?" She said that because she felt so sorry for him being in

such a state with his ears, she didn't have the heart to ask him what happened! That was useful, wasn't it?

"Did he seem to be in pain with his long ears?" I asked my sis. I was concerned for him. After what happened to me early in my life, I'm very close to Dr. Nik and I would have no hesitation putting in a good word for anyone in need. I was also trying to imagine this creature like a cat with long ears. I was trying to think. Mr. Poodle next door has long ears as well and he looks so silly, poor thing, I was trying to imagine a cat with ears like Mr. Poodle.

My sister added, "Don't say anything to anyone, but I think his mum washed him and then left him on the washing line for too long, hanging from his ears, and that's why he was there to see Dr. Nik." Black said that she went around his basket a couple of times because she wanted to find out what happened to him but couldn't find anything else wrong with him, just his short legs and long ears.

"Did you get his name?" I asked her.

"I already told you he wasn't talking to me, so how could I get his name? Anyway, what do you want to know his name for?" she said. I wanted to know his name because by then I was most concerned about this creature and I was ready to go and see mum. I wanted to have a word with mum about this creature that in my opinion was in serious need of help.

I added, "You saw mum and his mum talking to each other, right?" "Yes."
"Then why didn't you ask mum to have a word with his mum so she could make sure he was OK?"

"The time went very quickly," Black said "and there was no time for me to ask mum." That's typical of a woman, they stay away from home for hours but then when it comes to talking about very important matters, they tell you they had no time.

Anyway, I was most concerned about the welfare of this creature and was on my way to see mum so that I could discuss it with her and see if she could perhaps telephone Dr. Nik and see him about this, when I heard mum saying to dad that "Black Gold was most intrigued today with Mrs. So-and-so's rabbit"!

I tell you, women! They can't recognise what's what! Here I was, most concerned by what my sister was telling me, and then it turned out to be a rabbit, not a cat gone wrong! I've got to organise an outing into the bush with my sister Black and teach her what's what in life!

Lots of best thoughts,
Sir Norman

59. Did someone say Kent Frozen Chick?

Hello,

I don't think I've impressed my sisters. Therefore, before you hear the story from one of those two, either Goody-Two-Shoes or the Queen Bee, I'd better tell you upfront what I did.

Mum took a frozen chicken out of the freezer on Saturday night. It was all wrapped up in its packaging and it was left on the kitchen top to defrost overnight. What's wrong with that, you might ask. Well, of course, it can't be as straight and simple as that.

We all went to sleep that night in our respective places, and we all had a good night's sleep. I'm a very early riser and I was up by 5am. I went upstairs to see mum and dad, walked all over them, you know, just to make sure they knew I was awake. Being a Sunday morning, I'm not sure they were all that impressed but I wasn't told off. No movement, so I decided to shout my lungs off and make everyone in the house aware that I was up.

Still no movement. It was obvious by then that on that particular morning I wasn't going to win the game. I went browsing in all the rooms and then went back downstairs. I was bored, terribly bored! And by that time, my stomach had started rumbling.

The kitchen was the obvious and logical next destination. I had a look at my sisters' plates to see whether, by any chance, they'd left any biscuits or any food of any shape or form. I knew it was a waste of time, but you never know. Nothing! I then decided to see what the plan for the day was likely to be, from what was left on the kitchen top. A chicken! Mum must want to roast a chicken for lunch then. I went closer, smelt it, nothing much! The packaging was still intact. Oh, well, I'll just have to wait, I thought, OK. I went back into the front room, with the chicken in mind.

After a little roaming around, I couldn't get that bird out of my mind and I had to go back into the kitchen! Initially, I just wanted to smell the bird, to get a 'taster' of what mum would give us for lunch. I smelt it and smelt it again, and again but, with the packaging, it was just wasting my precious time.

I decided to open the wrapping. You know, I'm pretty good at that, I just slit the cling film with my claw and the job's done! So I did that! Now I'd released the aroma of tender chicken meat that would roast to its most succulent flavour for our lunch. I was looking forward to it, as a matter of fact, I couldn't wait! So much so that I said to myself, "Mum won't mind, I'm sure, if I have a little taste of it," and I did!

I slit through the cling film, just near the wing. You know how poultry wings are folded around the body once they've been packaged, so one of the wings was so tempting, I just had to have a go at it!

I was very quiet on the kitchen top chewing through this bird's wing and I was concentrating so hard that I didn't hear mum coming down with my two sisters. I was caught in the act! My mum started laughing. (And I might add, it's an achievement to make her laugh in the morning, she's one of those people who shouldn't be spoken to before her tenth coffee.) My sister Black looked at me as if to say, "Just like him" and my sister Pirate was totally, utterly horrified. Mum took a closer look at it, and the entire top of the wing had disappeared! I was good though, because I never damaged the rest of the chicken, so mum could cut off the bit I'd chewed and roast the chicken.

When it was lunchtime, my dad called everyone saying, "Wing-less bird is about to be served." I kept a low profile and just waited to be served my roast chicken! When mum put our three little plates on the floor for us, you should've seen the look I got from my sisters. I just remained very casual, as if nothing had happened. I had my lunch and thoroughly en-joyed it! I will try and behave better in future.

Much love, see you soonest,
Sir Norman

60. I'm checking on mum

Hello,

I've got to tell you something. I'm putting to good use all the education I was given and good manners I was taught at Wild Berry, yeah, truly. I'll tell you all about it now. I'm making sure that mum does the right thing. Dad calls me mischievous, very, very mischievous, but I'm not in trouble, they all had a good laugh! Mum put all the washing in the washing machine. She never started the programme and she didn't close the door, which suited my intentions just fine, then she left the kitchen.

I was still there after mum left and as I had nothing really important to do I thought I'd make myself useful by checking on what mum had put in the washing machine. I wanted to make sure she hadn't mixed colours with whites, so I got everything out. It was heavy work, you know, because there was big stuff in there, my dad's jeans, big bath towels, it was real hard work. The washing machine isn't that close to the ground, so I had to stand on my back legs and stretch to get to everything!

Anyway, I'd almost finished doing my duty when I got caught. I was asked what on earth I was doing. That was a bit of a silly question, don't you think? It was clear that I was putting my time to good use and making sure that mum was doing the right thing, and all they could do was laugh! Would you have laughed? I tell you!

I'll speak to you when I'm in a better mood,
Sir Norman

61. I get my confidence, while mum
gets a conference call

Hey, listen to this. I'm so happy, I've got lots of confidence now. Sorry, I'm so excited, I forgot to say hello to you all, I hope all's well with you.

You remember I told you that there's a bully black tom cat that comes into our garden? Remember? I heard mum telling dad that she asked Nico how dangerous it would be for my back legs if I ever got into a fight with him (now, come on, I'm not talking about getting into a fight with Nico, I'm talking about getting into a fight with the black cat that trespasses in my garden!) I know mum and dad were worried about this because I really don't like that black cat, he's so arrogant, you have no idea!

The other afternoon it happened that everyone was indoors, dad was downstairs working on his laptop and mum was upstairs. She was talking on the telephone. I knew she was expecting an important phone call that day, I heard her telling dad all about it. I knew myself it was really important because she wasn't talking normally, she was talking funny, so I knew immediately it was that important. Funny language means important business to me. So, dad downstairs, mum upstairs, me and my sisters outside. Mum happened to look out of the window while she was on the phone and, oh dearie, dearie me, the black cat was in the middle of the garden! I could see and hear mum. With one hand she was holding the phone to her ear, with the other hand she was opening the window and gesticulating wildly. I guess she meant to chase the black cat off, but it didn't work! Mum ran downstairs to see dad, still talking on the phone of course! She started making huge signals to dad so that he'd understand what she wanted. You know blokes, it took him quite a while to get the message, by which time mum had run out of patience, so she went out into the garden herself, still speaking that funny language of hers.

Finally the penny dropped for dad and he too was outside trying to stop me. The more they tried to stop me the more I was shouting at the black cat. You should have seen mum, what a laugh, if only the people on the other side of the world could've seen her. She was talking business and at the same time running around the garden, waving madly with her free arm in order to separate us, and I was shouting, and dad was running after the lot of us.

My dad made mum understand that he'd take care of everything, she could relax. From the look she gave him, I'm not sure she believed him but she had to go back upstairs, the phone still glued to her ear. I tell you, good thing there's cordless phones. In no time mum was back at the window looking to see what was happening to us. My sisters were just passively looking on!

You know what? I chased that black cat all the way to the bottom of the garden and then I made him jump over the fence, yeah, truly, I did! My fur had doubled in volume and my tail was as big as a tree trunk. Ooooh, I was annoyed with him, very annoyed, but I chased him off, and he never attacked me! Mum and dad know he attacks a lot of cats in the neighbourhood but he didn't touch me! I'm so proud of myself, and I got a lot of praise from mum and dad.

As usual dad got a good ear bashing. "I can't believe you

189

couldn't just look and see what was happening in your own garden," I heard mum telling him in a not-too-happy voice. She really had a go at him. Dad was trying to tell her that we didn't fight after all but mum wasn't having any of his explanation.

Dad told mum, "Good job that wasn't a video conference you had, girl."

I thought you'd be pleased to know that I'm not scared of anyone and that I defend my territory and sisters quite well now. Since that episode, I've had a lot of work to do, going around all over the place in the garden, spraying everywhere to say it's my territory!

Much love,
Sir Norman

62. Eat the turkey – said Pirate

Hello all,

I wanted to tell you about Pirate. I know I always say she is like the Queen Bee but I have to admit she's a good old dear to me and I'm getting to love her very much. Having said that, I always loved my older sister Pi but it was her that didn't want to know about me!

My sisters and I are developing a huge amount of love for each other, we play a lot and we're now great buddies! However, my sis Pi is getting very protective of me and she's teaching me lots and lots of things. I already told you that she's worldly wise and knows how to live well, so I just do as she tells me, and this is just what happened at Christmas!

I told you that on Christmas day we all had turkey. It was really nice white meat and I had a feast with my sisters. After the big day, there was quite a bit of that bird left over and I heard dad saying that it would make some really yummy sandwiches. While dad was saying that I noticed that both my sisters were licking their chops, so I went up to Black and asked her, "Do you know something I don't?" Black looked at me as if I were really thick, you know one of her à la Goody-Two-Shoes looks. Eventually she told me that every time mum makes sandwiches she usually gives us some cold turkey as well. Good to know, I said to myself.

The day after, out comes the bird, and mum started preparing the sandwiches, all according to plan! Both my sisters were on standby waiting for some meat and out of the cupboard came our three little plates. That was a really nice sound, and I was very excited! "Places!" mum called. She always says "Places" when we're about to be fed! We got served and I was very, very excited about getting some more lovely turkey!

Oh, dear, what's that? It's not the same colour as we had previously. I smelt it, the smell was yummy, but it just wasn't the same, I was getting worried. I looked at Black, she was eating. I looked at Pirate, she was eating as if she hadn't had a meal in two weeks. I took a look at my plate again, but it just wasn't the same as on Christmas day! I sat there feeling so sorry for myself. Pirate saw me and stopped eating, looking in my direction but guarding her plate as if it was treasure! She looked at me for quite a while and then all of a sudden she asked, "Well, boy, what's the matter with you? Why aren't you eating your turkey?" I looked at her and looked at my meat again but it just didn't look right to me.

You'll never guess what Pi did for me!

She could see I wasn't used to the meat. It was my very first time. It was turkey all right but it was the darker part of the meat, which I'd never had before. Pirate put a piece of meat in her mouth from her plate and looked at me. She didn't eat the meat, she just looked at me, with the piece of meat in her mouth, just to show me that she was having it. I looked at her, then she chewed it.

She put another piece of meat in her mouth and again, she looked at me with the meat in her mouth. I looked at her most intrigued and smelt my plate again, then looked at Pi who was chewing her mouthful. Pi stood there and looked at me and then said, "Now then, are you going to eat? You can

192

see that we're eating it. EAT YOUR MEAT!" she said, in a very domineering voice. By then, I was almost convinced that the meat was OK. I risked trying some and it was really nice, very tasty. From time to time Pi looked at me while finishing her meal. She was looking at me, making sure I was all right. When she finished her meal, she passed by me and said, "You stick with me and you'll learn all about the good life, brother!"

Since that little episode, every time mum gives us some new food (like tonight, for instance, we were given sardines), every time Pi looks out for me and I watch her to see if she's eating. If she is, then I'm reassured that what I'm being given is good for me!! For sure, I'll stick with the old girl!

Lots of good thoughts,
Sir Norman

63. The brushing session

Hello, it's urgent, please.

When I was living with you at Wild Berry and undergoing my training in how to behave in society, no one prepared me for something that came as a terrific shock!

Pi and Black were done at first while I was around and just looking on. I wasn't done initially, but it soon changed! I wasn't aware that I had to undergo brushing and grooming sessions and titifying as my dad calls it! Have you ever gone through this? No? Well, let me tell you all about it now!

I was first introduced to the matter very gently. Mum thought she was conning me. Hey, hey, come off it, dear lady! She'd make sure I was around while she brushed my sisters. I couldn't understand the need for such an activity, and to this day, I still can't understand it.

My sister Pi shouts all the way through the rigmarole. My sis Black, of course she likes titifying so she behaves better! So here we go with mum brushing and brushing and then spraying a mist of water and then stroking with a cloth, oh dearie, dearie me. I didn't think much about it, I told myself, "Well they need to be done, they're girls. No wonder people always comment on my sisters' coats, how very shiny they are."

Then one day, after she finished with my sisters, mum put me on the chair. "Oi, lady, what do you think you're doing?" I asked my mum. I realise this isn't the way to speak to your mum but, hey, I had to take control, there was no way I was going to go through that ordeal, no way. Mum took the 'instrument', I was looking at it from the chair and thinking that if she came any closer to me with that thing, I was going to be mad at her. I was warning mum, "Don't come any closer, or there'll be trouble." I was moaning and cursing, I was determined not to give in. "Don't come any closer."

I repeated myself. There was so much kerfuffle that dad appeared from upstairs. "I believe," he was telling mum, "I believe the boy is telling you that he doesn't want to go through it." I was very relieved to find dad defending me, but when he heard mum's response, the guy just left! I couldn't believe it, she gave him one of her looks and the bloke walked away from me! As he was leaving he said, "Sorry mate, I tried" What do you mean you tried?

"Oi, come back here, I don't want to go through this, I don't need all this fuss with my coat." While I was calling dad to come back, I got really mad at mum, and I scratched her hand. I'm very sorry, truly, I never meant it, sorry mum. I got away with it but that only made her more determined to have a go at my fur. She brushed me once, twice, but I was shouting so loud, I think I impressed her because she gave up! I thought, that did the trick and she won't ever do it again! WRONG!

I was put through this ordeal several more times, on different days. I thought at least if she could do it on a regular basis, on a Monday for instance, that would give me a chance to hide. Every Monday I'd disappear and that'd do the trick. No such luck. Mum would do it on the spur of the moment!

My sisters were done and then me. Not for as long as my sis-

195

ters, just a few strokes, but nevertheless, mum was having her say!

I thought if I carried on shouting, she'd give up sooner or later. Wrong again! Wrong until today. I had to go through the entire thing. She's got the knack now, mum has. She puts a hand firmly on my neck and then bingo, she starts brushing, then out with the water mist. I still shout but I can't be as mad to mum. Remember I told you she's Italian? When she loses her temper, boy, I'd better behave!

Anyway, now that I've told you all about it, I also want to tell you that I really don't like being titified and never will.

I'm thinking of you but I'm really annoyed,
Sir Norman

64. I thought I could help myself

Good morning all,

I've been naughty! And before anyone tells you anything, I thought I'd better let you know.

Besides football, my other passion in life is biscuits! I like them so much! Mum buys them in large bags. She buys chicken, rabbit, and salmon from the shop and then she orders the special ones for Black Gold. I like them all but particularly the ones that Black needs to have, I just love them!

Mum stores the biscuits in the larder and it's shut so there's no way I can reach them! The ones we need for the week, mum keeps them in jars in the kitchen, all labelled 'rabbit', 'fish', 'chicken' and 'Black Gold's Own'. Often I jump onto the top where the jars are stored to see if I can get at some of the biscuits but the lids are tightly shut and there's no way I can open a jar.

The other day mum got the special biscuits for Black and she came home and filled the jar. Then she had a phone call. There was no time to secure the bag in the larder, because she needed to answer the phone, so she temporarily put the bag of biscuits on top of the fridge.

Yeah, I know, you guessed already! I had to climb on top of the fridge and I made it alright. I spent quite a bit of time chewing a corner of the bag, it was so very tempting, I couldn't resist! I managed to get my teeth through one corner. It was hard work, because the bag is so thick, but I managed!

I was found lying next to the bag of biscuits, on top of the fridge. My dad found me up there! He started laughing, and called mum and I heard him saying to mum, "You should know better." As usual, I got away with it, I wasn't reprimanded but there are fewer and fewer things lying around. Mum always has to remember to secure everything because of my tendency to pinch things!

Speak to you soonest,
Sir Norman

65. Does anyone know where she is?

Hello there,

I'm writing to you because I've been left on my own and I feel melancholic. Well, the truth is that I'm not on my own, my sisters are with me and my dad too but today I miss mum and I wanted to tell you all about it.

I told you before, mum works from home, so we spend lots of time together, and we speak to each other a lot. OK, the truth is that I'm the one that speaks to her a lot. I also very much like taking part in conversations, so whether she's on the phone or simply talking to dad, I always express my opinion from the depths of my lungs.

I saw her putting her coat on, then her boots (there's snow outside and it's very cold), then I heard the door go, but before I could make it to the door she was gone! I jumped onto one of the dining chairs, then onto the dining table so that I could see where she was heading to, but I wasn't quick enough and I missed her.

There was nothing else I could do but wait for her to return. There was no point me going out into the garden to try to follow her, the fence and the gate are far too high and I can't jump that high (as yet).

Don't know why but today I was a little bit distressed. I can't explain it, I just wanted mum to be with me and not go out, I miss her. I lay on the dining table for a while waiting for her to return but I couldn't rest, so I went to see my sister Black in her basket, then I went to see my dad. He knew, my dad knew exactly how I felt. I went walking across the room like a lost soul and then jumped back onto the table, facing the window so that I'd be able to see her as soon as she returned, and I hoped she wouldn't be long.

All of a sudden, I heard steps coming through the front garden. There's ice on the ground, so I was lucky because it's quite noisy. I got up and looked through the window. I couldn't see that well because the sun was shining and, what with the glare from the snow, it was quite difficult to see well. I moved a bit along the table, quite restless now, but I still couldn't see. Who could it be?

I was so relieved, there she was. I could see her well now and any minute I would hear the key in the door and then she'd be back with me.

When mum got in I couldn't help but shout at her, I was so pleased she was back. I heard my dad telling her, "Sir Norman's been tap dancing on the dining table since you left, he kept on looking through the window for you." There was really no need for him to tell her that, no need at all.

I'm really happy now. I jumped off the table and stroked her leg as I went by. Now I can go back to sleep in my armchair.

Much love,
Sir Norman

66. Who did it?

Hello,

I've got something to tell you. Ssshhhhh, it's a secret!

Something happened the other night. It's a bit naughty, I'm going to try and explain it to you without too many details so that no one gets offended. It's a story about something that everyone does, two-legged and four-legged creatures alike, but no one likes to talk about it.

We were all sitting down watching TV, dad in his armchair, mum in hers, Pirate was occupying the three-seater sofa all alone, and I was on the back of mum's armchair.

Everyone noticed but no one dared say anything. Everyone was looking at everyone else. No words were said, everyone grew more and more suspicious, looks were flying around the room.

Everyone was pretending that nothing had happened, and looking elsewhere around the room, avoiding any eye contact. Everyone was pretending it hadn't happened except, of course, for my dad. Mum's always saying to him, "talk about discreet!" Gee, "Who did it?" shouted dad.

It couldn't have been me, I was lying half on the back of the armchair and half on mum's neck, it couldn't have been me. It wasn't mum, I'm sure of that, I would have noticed. For sure it wasn't dad, as he was the one who shouted. But in any case, it wasn't coming from his side of the room. And it couldn't have been Pirate. All eyes turned to Black Gold. She was very quiet in her basket, looking regal as always with her bottom lip showing; it looked like she had lipstick on.

"Black," said my dad, "you couldn't possibly?" She looked really ill at ease.

"It can't be her," Mum interrupted dad. And I thought to myself, Black is the princess of the house, she can't, for sure. Mum added, "Surely, you can see she's so pretty, look at her, do you really think that beautiful creature could do such a thing?"

Boy, oh boy, you can't even start to imagine the smell!

Bye for now, don't say I told you, it's a secret!

Speak soonest,
Sir Norman

67. I thought seats were allocated for life

Good morning,

How are you doing? I'm writing because I wanted to check a certain fact of life with you, so that if it happens again I'll know what my legal rights are.

I understood that armchairs were allocated for life. Can you tell me whether I'm correct or not? Actually, don't bother, because I know perfectly well that I'm correct! When I first moved into this house, after a few days I felt completely at ease and I put my stamp on areas that I consider mine, entirely mine. I don't expect anybody else in this house to change their mind and use what's mine, do you understand?

One armchair near the sliding door is mine for daytime purposes. It's supposed to be dad's but it's mine. It allows me to look outside and keep track of all the birds in the garden. It allows me to sleep as well, and I have my siesta there every afternoon, but if there's ever any noise outside, I'm right there on the spot, ready to look outside, without losing any time.

The other armchair is mine as well for nighttime purposes. It's mum's armchair and I sleep on it at night. It's very comfy and I can smell mum's perfume all over it.

So is that all perfectly clear?

The other day, dad had his lunch on my armchair near the sliding doors. I went mad at him! I jumped up and down all over the room, I rushed like mad all around him and the armchair, I jumped up at mum's plants behind dad. You know what? The bloke couldn't understand what I was trying to say! I mean, sometimes I feel like saying to him "Hey, dad, the lights are on, but no one's home."

Even with all this song and dance going on around him, the penny never dropped! He had to call mum, "This kid's behaving weird," he told her! Me, behaving weird? I mean, you're on my property and you dare say I'm behaving weird?

Mum stood there for a while. I was on the floor near dad and my armchair, looking at mum, then at my armchair, then at mum again.

"Get off that armchair," she said.

"What?"

"Get off that armchair, I tell you, that's what he wants."

"What?"

"You're in his armchair and he doesn't like it, he probably needs a little sleep and he wants the armchair".

Dad was moaning! "I can't believe this," he said, "I can't have my lunch in peace in my own armchair."

"This is no longer your armchair."

As dad moved out of the armchair, I jumped in. Mum said, "It's as simple as that." I'm so glad that someone in this house has some brains and knows exactly what belongs to whom!

You do agree, don't you? When you move into a house, you choose what's most suitable for your needs and that's it, it's for life, right? The people of the house subsequently have no right whatsoever to claim anything back, correct?

I'm glad that you confirm that!

See you soon,
Sir Norman

68. The Magnificent Four

Good afternoon,

I don't think I've ever told you anything about the Magnificent Four, have I? Very quickly, I'll tell you all about them now.

They're in the kitchen. That's where they live. They stand there, beautiful, full of pride, disciplined like a small army, inaccessible.

I've often lurked around them. It's particularly tantalizing that they live on the kitchen counter where I take my meals. I often contemplate trying to access them, get close to them, but to no avail.

Three of them are identical, but one is even more magnificent than the other three. Their tops are always perfectly in place. I've tried so many times to get their tops off; impossible.

I stare at them so very often, I even speak to them occasionally. I often brush my moustache against them. I'd like to think they're my friends!

They are the biscuit jars! Three of them have biscuits for all of us, one has Black Gold's special biscuits, although mum lets all of us have some of them too.

Magnificent!
Much love,
Sir Norman

69. Please put the goggles on – dad's DIY-ing

Hello to you all,

I'm writing to you today because I don't really know where to hide in the house or even in the garden, as my dad's decided to embark on some DIY today.

You've no idea how very painful this is for all the family, and if you were thinking of visiting, I'd advise you to put protective goggles on and, if you have them, then please put your sunglasses on as well.

Disaster on two legs, that's my dad when he decides to do DIY. Hopeless, that's the adjective that should be applied when talking about him and DIY. You don't believe me? I'll tell you a secret right now just to prove it (but don't tell anybody else I told you, right). In the house there are some plant pots and decorative pots and ceramics that stand alone. Do you know why they're there? They're to hide all dad's past DIY blunders, truly! When you come here, I'll show you!

I'm exhausted just at the thought of seeing all the mess around the house, tools all over the place! An example: a cupboard door needs a hinge tightened. Dad will clear out the whole cupboard, then remove the door, then try to dismantle the kitchen top. Disaster on legs, I told you!

I was playing in the hallway and my toy went behind some nice ceramic pots so mum had to move them so that she could get my toy back. Do you want me to tell you why the ceramics are there? To hide the mess that dad made when he laid the hardwood floor, you should see the corner!

Things get so bad when dad decides to DIY. Like today, for instance, everyone disappeared, my sisters went upstairs, I personally went under the bed.

Now, my dad's latest brilliant idea is that the hallway needs redecorating! My mum's jaws dropped. Once she recovered from the shock, she said to dad, "With you and Sir Norman in the house, plus redecorating? NO WAY!"

You tell me, what have I got to do with it? I don't understand this attitude. Mind you, on second thoughts …

It's now evening, dark, and my dad's still messing about with the cupboard hinge. He's cursing his screwdriver and whatever other tools he's using. They're never the correct size of course and now he says that maybe it's better to change the hinges altogether.

The saga continues, I'll let you know the outcome!

See you when I come out of hiding.

Sir Norman

70. Pirate's personal fitness trainer

Dear all at Wild Berry,

I'm keeping you informed about my life, as I promised I'd do when I moved out of Wild Berry but lately I forgot to inform you of a very important development. And so that's why I'm writing today.

Pirate is losing quite a bit of weight! Can you guess why? I make her run in the garden a lot! I heard mum and dad comment on how much weight the Queen Bee has lost, not only on her legs and back but also from her face.

It's simple; it's called exercise! Before I came here, Pi was used to a very quiet life – sleeping, eating and getting cuddles were the most important things in her life. Now, every time she goes into the garden, I make sure I'm behind her, and we play a lot – at hide and seek, for instance. Then I follow her wherever she goes and sometimes she wants to lose me, but I always find her, so she really gets lots and lots of exercise!

The other day dad told me that I'm a good boy and he asked me to keep on working out with Pirate! I felt very proud to be given the responsibility for such a task.

You'll see what I mean next time you meet Pirate!

Best thoughts,
Sir Norman

71. The temptation was too good to resist

Hello my friends,

Oh oh, I did it again! I've been naughty.

I've been cheeky with Pirate, but it was too good to resist. She isn't talking to me now but I wasn't told off by mum or dad. On the contrary, they laughed, so Pirate isn't talking to them either.

Mum and dad were having a coffee break. I was outside on the patio with my two sisters.

There was a lot of wind this morning, I mean real, terrible, gale-force wind. Everything had been blown and scattered around, the outside table was upside down, pots were over-turned, etc. One of the big containers for dead leaves was on its side, it had been blown from one side of the garden onto our patio. Scary; good job none of us were outside at the time! However, it created the best hide and seek toy for Pirate and me.

We played and played for quite a while, running around the empty container. Getting in and out of it was proving to be a really good game, as it was on its side. We took it in turns to go in and out of it, and then running around it again.

I can run faster than Pirate, there's no doubt about that. I'm fast enough to run around the container, go somewhere else in the garden and come back, and Pirate will still be going around the container! So I did just that this afternoon.

The thing is, when I got back to play with Pirate at the empty container, she never saw me coming. At first she was looking for me but then she sat there and she seemed completely lost without me! She was very quiet and I was behind her; big mistake with someone as cheeky as me! So I took advantage of it … I jumped on Pirate's tail and I bit it!

The old girl jumped ten foot high and then she turned back towards me. Gee, she was mad at me!

I ran as fast as I could. "Catch me if you can," I told her.

Lots of purrfect love,
Sir Norman

72. So much trouble

Pssssssssss, it's me!

Me, Sir Norman.

Ssssshhh, don't make a noise, don't speak so loud.

I'm in so much trouble, yeah, I am. Shhhhh, don't make it any worse!I've never been in this much trouble before. I thought I'd been in trouble before but never like today. Trouble is coming out of my ears, and not only that but coming out of every single hair on my body. I'm in such a pickle, you've no idea, man!

Just now, my dad said I shouldn't remind mum of my little four-legged existence, that's what dad said! At first I didn't want to believe him and I tried to get round mum, I went to see her, tried to talk to her, looked at her with big, loving eyes. But, gosh, nothing worked, man. On the contrary, I was just making her madder!

Dad told me again to go into hiding for a while, and this time I took his advice seriously. I went behind the sofa, and didn't come out for a few hours. I thought that was more than enough, so I ventured out a few minutes ago and went to the kitchen. Mum was in there working on something and I stood on the kitchen top, where I usually have my meals. I looked at mum with my big soppy eyes but, holy moley, she picked me up, walked to the front room and put me on the armchair, instructing me not to move. Man, I have no idea how I'll get out of this one! The old girl is raving mad at me! I never heard her shout till now but, boy, she did today! My dad told me that she was really, but really, mad at me, and he said I should believe him as he has lots of experience in the matter. As it's the weekend, I'm thinking about coming down to Wild Berry to spend the next couple of days there. I firmly believe it will be in my own best interests. You have a little cage for me, right? I'll bring my own biscuits with me, don't worry about feeding me, I'll be self-sufficient. I just need a place to hide and allow mum to forget about me for a couple of days. Yeah, it's that bad!

What did I do? Well, I'm very eager to show the entire world that my legs are now in perfect working order, so to start with I want to show mum and dad what I can do. So yesterday mum was away for the day and I was all alone with my dad in the garden, my sisters were indoors. I was helping my dad. He was cutting the overgrown ivy from the fence, quite a big job I might tell you! So while dad was busy, I was busy too, super-vising the place. I wanted to take a good look at the fence and I just jumped up onto it, and was walking along on it. I thought nothing of it really!

When my dad saw me up there, he said a word that I can't repeat here, and came over to me. "What on earth do you think you're doing up there, mister?" he asked me. He then tried to pick me up off the fence. He stood on an old tree trunk and as he got me in his arms, the trunk collapsed. I never felt in any danger at all. Dad had my little body under control all the time, but the only thing is that, in doing so, he did his back in.

When we told mum all about this in the evening, she started getting very annoyed with the two of us. She said, "Leave two blokes together for a few hours and pandemonium breaks loose." I heard her afterwards having a real go at dad; he's always in trouble for one thing or another.

As if yesterday wasn't enough, when mum left this morning she told dad to make sure I was kept properly under control.

"Yeah, yeah, don't worry love."

The day went on without too much incident. We had to be extra vigilant not to do anything wrong, BUT, when mum came back a little while ago, she caught me in the act. There's a gate, from the gate you can venture out. The gate is six feet high, I jumped on top of the gate, from the top of the gate, I jumped onto the other side.

The only thing is, that the other side is the front garden.

I could hear mum unlocking all the gate locks, then all of a sudden the gate opened wide and there she stood. Holy moley, I didn't know whether to run for my life, or just stay there not moving and hope that maybe she wouldn't see me!

She wasn't shouting but her look said it all. I didn't run away and mum was telling me with a very calm voice to go back inside the gate, which I eventually did. Once I was safely inside, I thought that all was forgiven. WRONG!

I could see mum locking all the security locks and I stood near her, because I thought she was going to tell me what a good boy I am. WRONG! Once she finished with the gate, she took a look at me and said, "INDOORS, NOW!" Do you know what? I certainly didn't need her to repeat the order! I

was off to the door like a rocket but then I relaxed once I arrived at the kitchen door. I was sure that by then the fresh evening air would have calmed her down.
WRONG AGAIN!

"INDOORS!" Holy moley, my mum never spoke to me like that before and to be honest I'd never heard her talking to anyone else like that either.

Once indoors, I ran to the front room to be near my dad. He was watching the news in his armchair and I sat by his legs. My mum came into the room and you could actually feel the wind arriving like a storm. "Oh oh," my dad said. Yeah, you could say that.

"What's the matter, love?"
"Don't you call me 'love'." Holy moley. I was looking at dad, then mum, then dad again.

"What's the matter?"
"Do you have any idea where I found him?"
"Who?"

"Him!" And my mum told dad everything, a bit as if it was all his fault that I jumped the gate. At first dad tried to take my side and point out to mum how exceptionally well I'm doing to be able to make such a big jump, but mum was having none of it. She was just raving mad at both of us! Now you know why I want to disappear from the face of the earth for a little while! Ssshhhhh, right now I'm going back behind the sofa.

Sir Norman

73. The ice cream matter

Hello dear all,

You might not believe what I'm going to say, but it's the truth! It's about Goody-Two-Shoes-Princess-Darling! She looks such a darling but she's just as bad as any of us! I tell you, man, she can get away with murder, with anything. You think she gets told off? No man, never!

It was movie time. My mum served ice cream; little tempting, appetising balls of yellowish, creamy delight. Naturally, dad is served in a bowl and my sisters and I have a small spoonful of the delightful stuff on our own plates. Mum is well organised, you know. We have plates for this and plates for that so, naturally, we have small plates for dessert purposes.

So we all had our share of bliss and that was that. Mum always sits down last, in the armchair, after everybody's been served and everything's in good order, so she did just that tonight. She had a small bowl with some of the stuff and started to have a spoonful, then a second one … Pirate was in her basket, Black Gold was in hers and I was in my dad's armchair. Then the telephone rings.

Mum puts her bowl on the rug, next to her armchair, gets up and answers the telephone. My sisters were asleep by then.

Mum had some business to discuss on the phone, so she went up to her study. She was only upstairs for about five minutes. In the meantime, her ice cream disappeared! When she came down, mum went to sit down again and picked up her bowl.

EMPTY! Black Gold was under the coffee table licking her chops! The little darling had not only eaten her own small portion of delight but she'd also eaten all of mum's. Dad was laughing and I was speechless. Pirate was so tired that she didn't wake up.

Black Gold sat licking her chops for quite some time, with the greatest satisfaction!

Mum sat in her armchair for a while without saying a word and then, she burst out laughing!

Not a word was said to Black! I bet you if that had been me, I'd have been in trouble big time!

See you soon,
Sir Norman

74. I am so fastidious

Good day,

Hope all is OK with you. I'm writing because one of you might know something about private matters, and might be able to advise me.

It's really very private, OK, so please don't say a word to anyone, it's just between you and me. It's a subject we didn't cover during my education at Wild Berry in my early days.

You know that I live here with these two gorgeous sisters of mine. I'm very happy and very well looked after, my sisters really love me now and we do everything together, like playing, going out and about, etc.

But there's one matter that remains very private to me. I'm a very outgoing personality but this really bothers me. You know, it's very private to my little person. Pssssssss, don't tell anyone, don't talk so loud, would you? I don't want to go outside. Someone might be watching, but indoors …

It's about, it's about using my tray.

Shhhhhh.

I can'tbear the thought of not being clean, and every time I use the tray, it turns out to be something like a full day's work for both me and my mum.

First, I'm so shy, that I have to wait till no one is around to go. Then, I can't help but dig and dig and dig again, as deep as I can. Finally, once my business is accomplished, not only do I spread the litter back onto the pit that I created but I also put plenty of other stuff into the tray, truly, everything that I can possibly find. That includes brushes, and bags and, if the litter bag's not too full, then I drag that into the tray as well. I can't help it, I find the whole private business so embarrassing, especially with my sisters around, I don't want them to think I'm not clean and a proper gentleman cat!

The only thing is that I have to roam around the house to see whatever I can find to cover the tray. Mum has already found a rug covering it. But the other day I went a bit too far. My dad left one of his shirts on the armchair and I took it from the front room and brought it all the way back to the tray. I thought that, this way, maybe my sisters would think that dad used the tray and not me.

I wasn't told off, though. I was just told that I had to stop doing such things. But how can I? You tell me. I'm so very fastidious about this business.

Can you please tell me how other creatures cope? What can I use to cover my tray? What can I use, if not the things that I find around the house? Would someone tell me, please?

This is a really worrying business, please advise me.

Hope to hear from you soonest,
Sir Norman

75. The bedsheet story

Good morning all,

Well, I'm not too sure it's a good morning after all. I need your help, I need it desperately. I need to find myself a little job, yeah, truly, I need to find one quick, very quick. I'm in so much in trouble, you have no idea.

I need to make some pocket money very quickly so, if you have any ideas or better still, a little job that I can do, I'll take it. I've learnt a lot of things lately, so there's nothing really that I wouldn't try. I'll turn my little paws to anything, I'm getting to be quite a little-boy-Friday.

Got to tell you what happened but you've got to promise me first that you won't say a word to anyone because it's quite a private matter. Ssssshhh, don't say anything to anyone, it's a bedroom story and, second, you'll help me out if you can find me a little job to make money very quickly so that I can get out of trouble. Promise?

Once upon a time my dad went to a far away country that produces the most beautiful and finest cotton in the world. He bought my mum the most beautiful bedlinen made with this finest cloth. It's so fine and delicate that the cloth is almost transparent, beautiful. The thing is that mum never wants to use this linen because she doesn't want to spoil it. Honestly, humans are difficult to understand. They have things and then they don't want to play with them or use them because they don't want to spoil them. So what's the point of having them in the first place? Anyway, because this

220

linen had been in the wardrobe for so long, mum decided to get it out and use it for a while so that she could air it and then put it back in the wardrobe. I really don't understand why human beings behave in such a fashion with their things, but that's what I heard mum saying, anyhow.

The point is that some months ago, I discovered a new game. Oh, don't worry, I still like football very much but this game is lots of fun too. I hide myself under the blankets or under the bedsheets and then I play and run in circles between the blanket and the sheets. I play and play until I'm completely exhausted. It's so much fun. Sometimes Pirate's on the bed as well and she looks at me as if I'm nuts. If mum tries to make the bed I get really mad at her. And if I go in the bedroom and find the bed in good order, I dig and dig, and pull the blanket and sheets until I can get underneath, it's so much fun. I get the cloth in my front paws and then I pull with my back legs and bite as hard as I possibly can with my teeth; great fun!

Now, then, I really need a little job to make some very quick money because I have been issued with an order to get a new set of bedlinen, made with the same cloth. The pocket money that I have right now will not suffice, I need more, a lot more. I've got to buy this new set of linen. Yeah, you got it. I made a big, but very big, hole in it. I never meant to, of course, but mum is so mad that she doesn't want to hear my explanations. I was playing, you see, and I got a little bit carried away. I heard mum telling dad that she can have it repaired but the repair will show because the hole is right on the top of the sheet, the part that shows. Can you help, then? If you hear of a little job, please, you know where to find me, right?

Lots of love from my hiding place,
Sir Norman

76. See you at some point, Pirate

Dearest sister Pirate,

Although everyone is indoors the house is silent, there's no sound. Outside there's a myriad birds but they're not singing. The trees that just yesterday were in bloom, today have for some mysterious reason lost all their flowers as the wind seems to be such in a terrible mood.

No one ventured into the garden this morning to check that everything was in good order. The greenhouse remains unopened, does it really matter today?

Black Gold has turned into a hibernating creature. Don't worry, she's well but isn't interested in anything or anybody around her. I tried to talk to her but she just spits back. I tried to interest her in going out, maybe even playing, but she's truly not with it and wants to be left alone. I understand her, after all these years.

Dad's pretending to read his newspaper. I jumped onto the sofa several times trying to attract his attention but it didn't work, and the newspaper is still upside down. Mum's doing the hoovering. Again. She doesn't realise that she must have done it three times already this morning. Everyone is bumping into each other but pretending it's not happening.

I don't feel like doing anything. I can no longer be your shadow. From you sister, I learnt everything I know today. I know we had some difficult times at first, but it was all because of your strong personality. You might have thought that

I wanted to take everything away from you. You soon realised that I didn't, and you then gave me everything. Black and I take it in turns to hide in the peonies, now time spent there doesn't need to be shared out three ways, just two. Wasn't it much better when we had to fight over it? Even the strawberries decided not to be ready for dad's birthday.

Just to let you know, sister, I'm looking after everyone and everything. I don't want you to worry about anything. I'm now able to put into practice everything you trained me to do. You can be proud of me.

Thinking of you, dearest sister. Today I even managed to catch my first bird ever, just today, just thinking of you.

Love you lots, big sis,
Sir Norman

About the autor

Antonella Cane was born in Alba, Italy, in the beautiful mountains near Turin where you find wild truffles growing deep in the ground. Her childhood was coloured by the ritual of digging truffles and the sounds of barking dogs. Her family owned lots of truffle-sniffer dogs – but no cats were allowed in the house!

Her family had business activities both in Italy and in the South of France, so she was raised with Italian and French as her mother tongues. Antonella studied in Paris at the Fashion Institute and later worked for the fashion house of Dior in Paris making exclusive one-off handmade evening gowns. Later, she used that experience to open her own successful fashion atelier in Monte Carlo under the name 'Antonella di Monte Carlo'. Antonella was frequented by society ladies and her evening gowns were often present in elegant events and noted in the press.

Antonella is active today as a textile artist and a consultant for textile-related export and investment, working for institutions such as the International Cotton Council in the UK and US Trade Boards (Mississippi and other projects). As well as for government promoted trade projects for Italy and France. She has also worked for projects for Africa (Senegal) and New Zealand.

She lives in Edenbridge, Kent and Robilante-Farm (in the mountains near the French-Italian border).

Antonella hopes that her Sir Norman the Cat stories will encourage more people to help animals in distress and also discover the joys of bringing a stray four-legged friend into their homes and hearts. If you have a cat story, please write to her – she would love to hear from you. (A.F. Sundberg)

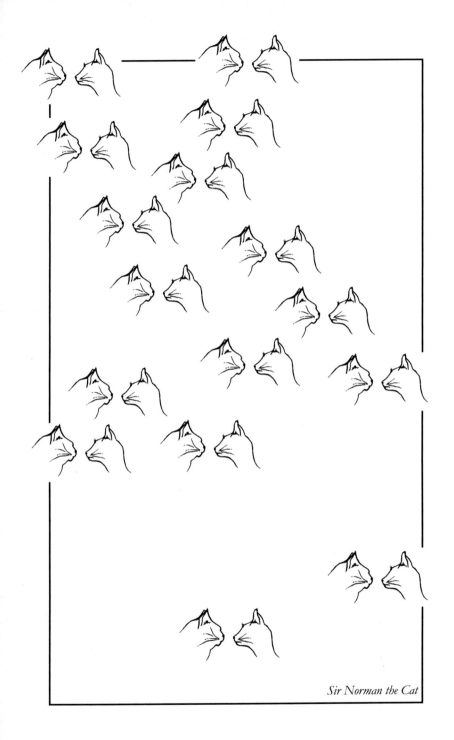

Sir Norman the Cat

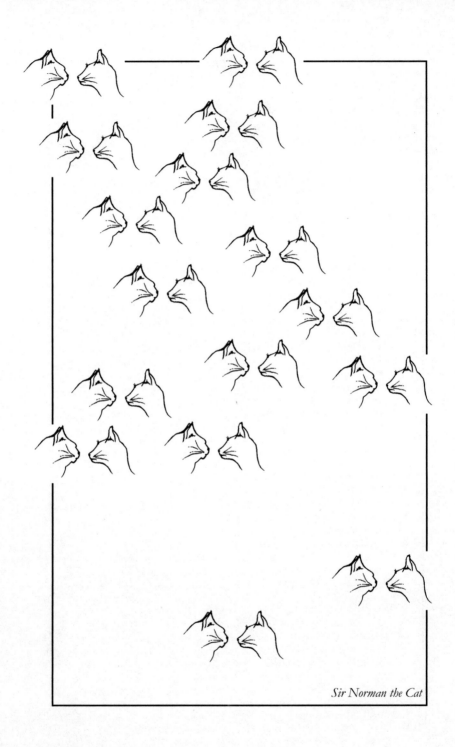

Sir Norman the Cat